I0597523

Disruption

Fiction Series
The Alex Evercrest Series
The River Front
The Girl on The Grill
Missing
Maggot
Racist
Votive Candles
Windy City
Country Road
Pool of Blood
Sins of the Daughter
Body Parts
The Skull Collector
The Vanishing
The Shadow Fighter
Moonshine
Grief's Trajectory
The Magic Touch
Northern Lights
Alex Evercrest Heroine
Alex Evercrest Collection Two
New Direction
A Family Affair
Disruption
The St. Lebuinnus Church Murder

A Brian O'Neil Novel
Hawaiian Phoenix
Moon Curser
Death Broker

The Problem Solver Series
Solutions
Drug Lords
Border Crosser
The Problem Solver Collection

The Taelo Series
Taelo: The Early Years
Taelo: The Golden Feather
Taelo: Journey of Discovery
Taelo: Dangerous Passage
Taelo: Condor Clan Slingers
Taelo: Circumvention
Taelo: The Journey of Sages
Taelo: Collection
Taelo: Future Leaders Journey
A Taelo Story:
White Swan and Quiet Pheasant
The Child's Name
Floating Cloud
Quiet Rabbit
Busy Bee
Little Otter & Talking Wren
Broken Spear
Burley Bear & Meadow Flower
Taelo Story Collection
Science Fiction

The Savitar Series:
Journey's End
Savitar
Confluence
Savitar Series Collection

Bram Nielson Series
The Fold
The Message
Fold Wormhole
Negative Fold
Ripples in Time
Bram Nielson Collection

<u>**Single Science Fiction Books:**</u>
Current Past and Future
The Event
The Door
Viajante 7

https://www.remwriter95.net/

Ron Mueller

Disruption

By: *Ron Mueller*

Around the World Publishing LLC
Cincinnati, Ohio

Ron Mueller

This story is a work of fiction. Names, characters, places, and incidents either
are products of the author's imagination or are used fictitiously. Any resemblance
to actual events or locales or persons, living or dead, is entirely coincidental.

Disruption ©

All rights reserved, including the right of reproduction, in whole or in part in
any form.

ISBN 13: 978-1-68223-931-5

Distributed by Ingram
Alex Evercrest Model By: Pi03@ShutterStock
Cover Picture by: Bill Lawson @ShutterStock
Cover by: Ron Mueller

Ron Mueller

1 The Call

*I*t's a bit unusual for a young daughter to narrate what her mother is doing. However, I am ten years old going on eighty and figured it was better to know what my mother was doing then naively sit by and act like a ninny.

I am Alex's adopted daughter, Aurea. I was born in Sao Paulo, Brazil to two wonderful parents. However, my wonderful father was a drug distributor.

Yea I know that is horrible but he was a great father.

When he fled and came to the United States, he thought that he had escaped to a new honest life but…he had not.

I learned that to protect me from the drug dealer that had traveled to the US to kill him, he and my mother left me on a stranger's porch. She was a stranger to them but they both knew her by the reputation she had earned as the leading police detective in Cincinnati. They never missed her reports when she made the news.

It was the only place they could think of where they could leave me and know that I would be safe.

They were running from the man sent to get them and had not been sure they would escape and…. they did not. They were killed but it would take months for me to find out.

They had not randomly picked any porch; they had picked the porch of a person they were sure would be able to protect me. It was Alex Evercrest's Price Hill home. Not only did she protect me, but she also dealt with the Brazilian drug lord and the person who had killed my parents.

Then in a move that forever changed my life as well as hers, she and her husband Matt adopted me.

I know now that they both love me.

My mother left a very successful career as the lead Detective in the Cincinnati Police Detective Unit so she could raise me in the house where she had grown up. She was able to set up her new detective service in Evanston, Illinois, which was within walking distance of the marina where her father had kept the boat that she and he had used to go out on Lake Michigan every Saturday morning. She bought the marina and the boat, the "Golden Goose."

We moved into the house that she had grown up in.

She, Matt, and I live on the second floor.

Her parents, Rose-Anne a very successful lawyer her father, Russel, a distinguished professor at Northwestern University live in one wing on the first floor.

We all share the great room, the kitchen, and the swimming pool.

Disruption

It is such a great place. I can swim in the pool every day and there is also a hot tub that is great to just sit in.

I thought of her as rich when I was put on the porch in Cincinnati.

When I saw the house she had grown up in I knew she had grown up rich.

When she solved her first case from her Evanston office and the business made close to a billion dollars.

I knew she was rich.

I am narrating this because I am an old child who is a mulatto girl born in Brazil, adopted by a family that is black but rich and go to an all-white school in Evanston, Illinois where I am determined to follow in my adopted mother's footsteps.

Let me say that I don't discriminate based on a person's skin color but see if they follow my mother's guidance of "treat others as you wish to be treated." And that means there are lots of people that I discriminate against.

So now you know a little about me.

I would like to focus on the impossible case that, Jane Stradford, the Illinois Lieutenant governor, the person that my mother considered an "Aunt," who also had my mother on retainer called to ask her to take on.

It was an impossible case, but my mother accepted the challenge of reducing the drug flow coming into the Chicago Area.

As was her habit she always followed the money and in this case the money flow was huge, and it was the most critical element.

It was also the element that would draw the most reaction from the four major Mexican drug cartels operating in Chicago.

So, you are going to be listening to this eighty-year-old, pre-teen as I narrate a story that blows my mind and pulled me in as if I was a fish that had taken the bait, hook line and sinker.

This case was a pivotal moment in my life!!!

*   *   *   *   *   *   *

The exchange of money for drugs along Independence Boulevard was on full display as Jane walked by with Police Chief, Jesse Franklin. He was informing her that more than one million one hundred thousand persons twelve or older had used illicit drugs in the Chicago area in the past year.

She learned that the primary drug markets were located on the South and West sides of the city in areas controlled by violent street gangs and what she was observing was just the tip of the iceberg. He let her know that the common drugs being sold were cocaine, marijuana, opioids, and methamphetamines. He added that marijuana followed by heroin were the two drugs sold in the highest volume.

She had requested the on the street tour , was shocked by the openness of the drug transactions and wanted to know why the police department was not out in full force arresting everyone that they were walking by.

The Chief shook his head and replied that he had tried that and then it became obvious that the bottleneck was that he had overloaded the judiciary and those arrested never got to court but had to be released. So now he had his men arrest pushers but only at the rate that the courts could process them.

She returned to her office and went to a meeting that was digging into the drug problem. Those present at the meeting were from the city and the communities in the surrounding area.

She knew that as long as there were customers there would be drugs flowing.

She had suggested a balanced program that arrested the buyers and the pushers and charged one for illegally buying and the other for selling. That had been a lead balloon that hit the floor as soon as she launched it.

She felt like she was getting an education on the drug business that she had thought she was on top of but in fact had learned facts and seen activity that made her realize that she needed to change the approach versus continue to sit in meetings and listening to complaints that seemed to have no solutions or suggestions that got no support.

In the meeting she learned that the drug traffickers were operating on the Dark web that is primarily used for illegal activities like selling stolen personal information, paying for an assassination, and trafficking in weapons and drugs. This she learned was a part of the internet that is hidden from the normal search engines and used to circumvent law enforcement.

She was introduced to the Tor and I2P browsers that was capable of browsing the Dark web and the use of Onion routing techniques that protected a user's identity by routing their information through many layers of relay points.

She also learned that intelligence agencies were active on the Dark web. She was introduced to the concept of the Clearnet that is comprised of most of the public websites that get visited during normal browsing of the internet and the concept of the Deep web also referred to as the Invisible web hidden from searches by the common commercial search engines.

She had learned a lot but had no idea of how to make a dent in the drug situation in the Chicago area.

During the meeting it was clear to her that continuing the effort to reduce the quantity of drugs being distributed in the Chicago area needed a fresh approach and an approach that would be able to follow the trail in the various realms of technology that enabled closer and secret communications such as the Activate My Line of Site (ALMOs) and the use of the Dark Web by the drug pushers.

She needed someone who could interact in the current challenging environment and do something concrete to change it.

She knew it was time to call her very capable "niece," Alex who had relocated to Evanston and had opened her own detective agency.

She remembered well that Alex had taken on an investigation that had stumped both the Canadian and US top police agencies.

Disruption

That was the case that was referred to as "The Sins of the Daughter," where Alex had worked across international boundaries to solve the case of a female serial killer. Alex had solved that case in record time after the other agencies had work for two years and had come up cold.

She figured that at a minimum the drug trade would take her to both the Canadian and Mexican border. She had confidence that Alex would figure out some sort of action that would be felt by the drug distribution community. She had no idea of how to provide any guidance but she did have Alex on retainer and she was going to ask her to do something.

In her office, Alex was sitting and reviewing the last few cases that Evercrest, McGregor, Smith and Obrien Partners, LLC had just closed. It had been a slow few months but she had enjoyed that time because it allowed her to be the "mother" to Aurea in a manner that let the two of them bond in the same way she had bonded with her parents.

When school was over the two of them would sit on the deck of the Golden Goose, sip on a root beer or orange soda, talk and do homework. If the Golden Goose was out on charter they would eat at the newly opened Golden Goose Restaurant, afterwards walk to the office, and do homework in one of the meeting rooms. She smiled as she thought that it was great that business was slow.

The call from Jane came somewhat of a surprise. From the tone of Jane's voice Alex knew that she was about to get activated. She was on a retainer with the state of Illinois via Jane's office.

She listened as Jane outlined the situation that she was facing with the flow of drugs into Chicago. She asked if Alex would take on the task of reducing the flow.

Alex was quiet for a moment. She was not contemplating rejecting the request but she was thinking about what she could do to make even a dent in the drug flow. She asked Jane how they would measure success of such an effort.

She pointed out that as long as there were people wanting to buy drugs, the flow would continue. She said that she wanted to engage her team and arranged a meeting with them for the following day to get their read on taking on such a case.

After the call she asked Marisa to set up a meeting with Trey, Johnnie, Linda, and Lorie with the objective to discuss a new case.

When the meeting started, Lorie said that she hoped that they would finally get a case with some challenge.

Linda laughed and reminded her that she might regret getting what she wished for. She reminded Lorie that she had asked for action on their first case and had been shot by the person they were tracking.

Johnnie joined in on the banter and said that he had a very lucky day when he had stopped the boss on her way to work. He had been wishing someone would listen to him. He paused for a moment and then in a sad voice said…"she did and look what had happened to him."

Lorie laughed and said that yes look at him now, one of the richest, black Vietnam veterans in the country.

Trey as always was the quiet one but he added that Alex had positively impacted all of them. He said he wanted to know what the case they were about to hear was all about.

Alex described the case they were being asked to handle as a case that had no long term solution.

As it became clear that they were being asked to disrupt the flow of drugs and confiscate as much of the cash flowing back to the suppliers of the drugs, Johnnie said that once he had the names of the individuals involved he would see if he could hack his way into their computers. He smiled and said that he would set up the door leading to the disruption of the cash flow and he would leave the shooting part for the rest of the team to enjoy because the voice of the drug cartels was usually heard as big bangs.

Alex nodded and agreed that the internet was going to be a key part of their investigation. She asked Lorie, who had also become an excellent hacker to partner with Johnnie. She then said that she, Linda, and Trey were going to keep their boots on the ground. They would investigate how the drugs were flowing in and how cash might be flowing out of the country. She added that she wanted the three of them to disappoint Johnnie and not do any shooting.

She asked Marisa to be their communications coordinator and keep everyone working together even when she and her team were out in the field.

Marisa smiled and said that she was being given the most difficult job and would be eating a lot of ice cream to keep down her stress.

She just loved working with everyone and felt great about being included in the planning.

Johnnie asked Lorie if she wanted to sit in his office and get set up to hack into bank accounts and other personal computer systems.

Alex asked Marisa to contact Jane's office and get the names of the most prolific Chicago area drug distributors. She was not looking for anyone distributing on the streets but was looking for the persons providing the drugs to the distributors. She wanted to take action against the top leaders.

Immediately after the team meeting she called Jane to let her know that her team had all agreed to take on the case and that she would be getting a call from her support for names and any other information that would help.

Harold was sitting in his office thinking about what he needed to have his team do next to at least slow the drug flow into the Chicago area including the vicinity around it when he got a call from Alex. His association with her had started long ago on the day he had watched a coal barge light the sky out over Lake Michigan and the person he met returning from a fishing trip in an small open fishing boat that she had rented to go out in. Since that day, every additional meeting seemed to be associated with the cases that got tougher but all that she eventually solved.

This time when she let him know that she had been requested to take some sort of action to reduce the flow of drugs into the Chicago area, a smile spread across his face.

He asked how he and his team might be of help. She also let him know that she had her whole team sitting with her to listen to their discussion. He greeted everyone and asked what kind of fun were they all going get into together.

Alex knew that Harold would be one of the people that would provide some details that would help her team get a foothold on what she saw as an ocean of drugs whose tidal surge made the shore hard to stand on. She asked if he would help her and the team by sharing some of the key people importing drugs into Chicago.

Harold said that he was sending the information of four top people as they talked who were doing the distribution and he also had several names of the people that were handling the money. That money went mostly back to Mexico but he also had two additional contacts that spirited the money through Canada and through China. He said that much of the Mexican cartel money flow was a physical transport of cash that they had always practiced and it took three forms.

He said that a common form was for a well-paid courier, usually a Latin American woman who boarded a plane with a prepared carryon suitcase or backpack packed with cash in the form of one hundred dollar bills.

This was hard to intercept because their carry on were packed so they would not trigger an inspection when they went through customs.

He added that his team was currently watching two women of Columbian and Mexican heritage who had made frequent trips in the last year and were suspected of transporting cash back to Mexico and to Columbia. He said that he had that covered and didn't need help there.

He then said that a good percentage of the money was distributed to different small companies. He provided the names of second hand car dealers that his group suspected. He added that many were relatives or friends of the drug distributors. They conducted their business in a cash only approach and simply overstated the number of cars sold and were thus able to put money into their bank accounts.

He added that he felt that a good hacker could deal effectively with those people and he did not want to know anything about how Johnnie might handle that area.

There was a moment of silence then he went on and said that the third area was the transporting the money via truck. The trucks that had delivered the drugs went back to Mexico loaded with cash. That was the way eighty percent of the money currently returned to Mexico.

Most of the other twenty percent went to Canada where it was then distributed through a series of small companies and eventually returned to the US as laundered money.

He added that in both cases, he, his team, and other law enforcement personnel were hampered by many of the laws that kept them from legally stopping the suspected trucks doing the transporting.

They could only stop a truck if they had direct evidence of smuggling that was in progress and that was a very hard criteria to meet.

He added that the reason that cash went back to the kingpin sending the drugs to the US was usually that it was needed to pay for the next shipment of drugs. Or in the case of the more old fashioned organizations, the leader wanted to have the money close at hand for any personal or organizational emergencies.

Harold then shared the fact that one of the cartels that had come to Alex's defense a couple of years ago against the Mafia was one of the top distributors of cocaine. He asked if that would be a problem for her.

Alex made a point that she had shot and killed the leader of that cartel.

She paused for a moment to take in everything that Harold had shared, then asked the team if they had any questions.

Johnnie shook his head, then asked who the IT contact was on Harold's team.

Harold said he would have him contact Johnnie, chuckled, and said that he wanted his IT not to break any laws.

No one else had any questions, so Alex closed the meeting by inviting Harold and his team to a fishing trip on the Golden Goose she said that a date would be set by Marisa.

After the call Alex looked around and asked if everyone had what they needed to start.

Johnnie and Laurie said that they were set and would be getting into the bank accounts of the people that Harold had identified. It might take them a few days but they agreed that they would be able to set up a door to those accounts and monitor from where money came and where it was sent. They would also get into the car dealer accounts and see if they were being used to launder the money coming from the drug business.

Linda nodded and said that it seemed that a few trips to the local car dealers would allow them to get a handle on what was happening there and that after that they could give Johnnie and Laurie the green light to get into their banking systems and take the actions that would divert the dirty money.

Trey suggested that they ask Harold for the names of the enforcers that the people they would be investigating used. Getting their pictures and information about their habits was important so the three who were going out in the field were prepared for potential confrontations.

Alex nodded and then reminded everyone to wear their Kevlar suits. They had not been doing so for most of their recent business but they were stepping back into the realm where the gun was often the primary communication protocol that was practiced. She then said that the meeting was over.

She asked Marisa to set up daily morning progress meetings then returned to her office.

1 The Call

2 Finding the Trail

*M*y mother is a person who always wants to feel the fabric of the clothes she is about to buy. Getting into a case always followed a series of activities that was like feeling the fabric.

Her actions were simple. She went to where the action was visible or could be detected. The drug use on the streets were so open that she wondered if the police were being bribed to look the other way. The cash flow was a matter that required the sophisticated and probably illegal actions that Johnnie the oldest person on the team, and Laurie the youngest person on the team were into.

Johnnie is an interesting old black Marine Vietnam vet who my mother rescued from the streets of Cincinnati. He is one of my mother's most ardent supporters though it is hard for me to discern differences in the support my mother has from any of the team that is with her.

Lorie is the youngest daughter of Annie who my mother rescued after her fifteen years of being chained in the forest of Pennsylvania. She was kidnapped by a neighbor who chained her in a cabin in the woods. The kidnapper was the father of both Linda and Lorie. Linda is the older sister and was named after Annie's mother. Both of them have always called my mother their "Aunt." They were my age when my mother was shot in the chest and neck by the man who had chained their mother in the woods. He did not survive my mother's reaction to being shot.

It really is a struggle for me to keep my focus on the case. You have to give me a break, after all, though I claim to be an old girl of eighty but I am biologically only ten and learning about the loyal people that surround my mother has been a challenge.

On this case Harold, the Chicago DEA Chief turned out to provide key drug dealer names, an education on the current types of drugs that were hitting the street and providing direct support. He and my mother have a long history of working together and for this case he was to have more impact than on most of her other cases.

I think the most interesting thing about his relationship with my mother was his naming a money sniffing dog Cathy which is my mother's middle name. The whole team loved it. It was a way that they all could periodically poke fun at her by poking fun at Cathy. I fell in love with Cathy because she was a fun dog and in the course of this case she ended up saving my mother's life.

But I am getting ahead in the order that I am explaining the case and will focus on the key points that I learned. The learning was not all linear, so I apologize if sometimes I get confused and lead you astray.

*   *   *   *   *   *   *

As was her habit, she decided to start the investigation on the streets of Chicago. Early in the morning she drove down to the lake front with three bikes on the back of her black antique Jaguar. She led the procession of three riders and rode the downtown streets. Her goal was to get a feel for the drug distribution activity. What she found let her know that a number of the police walking the streets must have been paid to look the other way or the number of arrests were so high that they had been told to reduce the arrest rate. In either case the distributors were openly plying their trade and the customers seemed relaxed at getting their supply.

She decided that she would need to have a meeting with the Chicago Police Commissioner and get an understanding of what the police were doing about the tremendous and open distribution of drugs. Her position within Jane's department was one rung higher than the Police Commissioner so she knew she would be able to schedule a timely meeting.

When they got back to the Jag, Trey commented that it seemed that the drug activity had increased since the last time they had taken a similar ride just a couple of years ago. He smiled and asked if they could have lunch at Harold's Aunt's restaurant.

Alex said that sounded like a great idea. She called ahead to see if they would need a reservation. She was greeted like she was the most favored of customers and was assured there would be a table for the three of them.

When they arrived, she was surprised to see Harold waiting at the door. He gave her a hug, shook hands with everyone, and said that he was not going to miss hearing how her new business ventures were both going. He said that he was called by his Aunt as soon as she had hung up. He smiled and said that his Aunt had a menu item that was named after Alex.

Linda shook her head and said that as always, her aunt was known and admired everywhere.

When Rachel, Harold's aunt came to their table she made a point of giving Alex a hug and welcoming her back. She added that Alex's fame and recent social work had a positive impact on her business and the Evercrest special was one of the top selling items on the menu. She added that her new customers had picked up her menu at the Evercrest Legal Office and told Alex to thank her mother.

Alex smiled and said that she surely could not order anything else. She asked what came with the Evercrest Special.

Rachel smiled and said that the special was an eight ounce porterhouse smothered in a blue cheese sauce, asparagus on the side and a small baked potato smothered in butter and for desert it was crème de Brulé.

She then added that all the iced tea they might drink was included and if they wanted non-alcoholic wine she had Lambrusco to go with the special.

She then laughed and added that some of the customers had asked why the wine was non-alcoholic and she always replied because the person that the special was named after was a non-alcoholic person.

Trey, Linda, and Harold all said that they were ordering the Evercrest Special and like her they would take the iced tea.

While they were waiting for the special Alex asked about the Police Commissioner.

Harold said that Jesse Franklin had been promoted to that position and was trying to have an impact on the drug use. He was after the users with as much effort as he was in trying to reduce the distribution but was facing a budget crunch issue and a court system that was overloaded. He was also facing some political resistance about arresting the users.

Alex then asked for more detail on how the cash flow was being handled.

Harold pointed out that the US had a highly sophisticated financial sector with rigorous oversight. This created a "push" factor that influenced the cash flow back out of the country. The money was regularly loaded onto trucks heading for the Mexican border and then across where it could more easily be banked and then put through a series of bank transfers that allowed the final account to be "clean."

It was a money laundering scheme that involved several off shore accounts and then when it got back into a US bank it was available to purchase stock on the stock market.

He then added that Myanmar, Iran, Venezuela, Syria, Mali, Mozambique, Nigeria, South Sudan, Guinea-Bissau, and Laos were the top ten countries where the money from the Mexican cartels were headed and were considered primary "pull" countries because of their weak financial controls. He added that Venezuela and Laos seemed to be the two that were used the most by the Chicago drug distributors. He added that many countries that are primarily cash based could also be places that were being used. He highlighted the fact that Peru was another country in the Americas that qualified. He then shared the fact that the cash flow was a multibillion dollar affair.

He went on to describe how various cartels, "stored" the funds in what they considered safe locations. He added that safe simply meant beyond the reach of the law or their drug cartel competitors. It also depended greatly if the cash was needed to pay for a further consignment of drugs. Often a cartel was being so successful that their ability to launder the money exceeded their laundering capacity or the laundering organizations could not serve the competing cartels. He made the point that the individuals involved with money laundering had skills that allowed them to migrated from one cartel to another which meant that a cartel might be caught with extra cash on hand because they were short of launders.

He then highlighted the fact that the cartels often branched out into other businesses where a different currency was not the dollar, and they needed access to a currency exchange facility. An example of that was the fact that Columbia operated on the Peso and paying for the cocaine that was sent north meant needing to change the US dollar into the Columbian Peso. This was often a money laundering bottleneck.

He made the point that purchasing property in the US was one of the reasons to support the money launders that existed in every state of the union. These money launders were often related to members of the various drug distribution networks or had been in one of their organizations and as they moved up in the organization they often went into the money laundering end of the business. This got them into safer positions and allowed them to raise a family.

Harold then smiled and said that he had a new member of his team, that he had named Cathy, she was trained as a cash and drug detection dog and was currently the top contributor to the recovery of illegal money. He had promoted her to the rank of Special Money Recovery Agent in Charge and made sure she had the best food to eat.

He shared a most recent confiscation of money that Cathy had been able to sniff out at a truck inspection station run by the Illinois Department of Transportation. They had called him and shared that they had a truck they suspected of smuggling but they did not have the authority for that kind of an inspection.

He and the team took Cathy out to the station, and she participated in a truck "safety" inspection. She was able to detect the money that was surrounded by one ton super bags containing ammonium sulfate. A physical examination of the forty supper bags revealed six block shaped packages. A total amount of eleven million dollars were found in the two trailers that semi was pulling. The truck was scheduled to head to San Diego where super bags were to head to Columbia.

Alex laughed and asked about the sniffer's name.

Harold smiled and said that Cathy's attitude and mannerism reminded him of a friend that he was very fond of.

Trey chuckled because he knew that Alex's middle name was Cathy. He added that he was looking forward to meeting Cathy.

Lunch arrived and the conversation turned to how good the food tasted. The blue cheese melted over the steak was one feature that elevated the taste to a very interesting and delicious flavor.

Alex complimented Rachel on the meal and said that she loved the porterhouse and the crème de Brulé would have her coming back as often as possible.

On the drive back to the office, Linda asked what approach they were going to take.

Alex replied that she wanted to get the entire team together and figure out what their end goal was going to be for the case. She then said that what the team decided was what she would share with Jane to see if it was sufficient for what she wanted to accomplish.

After that they would work together to develop a plan that would deliver the goal they set together as a team. She added that Johnnie's and Lorie's hacking skills would be a key element of any plan and physically disrupting the flow of cash would be another. She added that she didn't think they would have much of a direct impact on the flow of drugs unless the loss of money disrupted it.

Trey shook his head and said that if one cartel was coming up short on importing drugs because their competition was short of cash they would almost instantly increase their flow. The demand was the key driver and the demand so far had never gone down.

Linda nodded and said that she was going to concentrate on how they might disrupt the cash flow. She chuckled and said that she had an idea on how to leverage using Cathy.

It was almost two when they got back to the office. Alex asked Marisa to schedule a meeting at eight the following morning. She then asked Trey and Linda to meet with her so they would be ready for the morning meeting. An hour later the three of them were clear on three objectives.

First, they would have Johnnie and Lorie disrupt cash flow via making it disappear from the bank and then get into the bank accounts of all the business's being locally operated to launder money.

Second they would disrupt cash being transported by tagging trucks being loaded with the cash and then creating the situation where the illegal money could be confiscated.

Third they would enlist Brian and Kekoa to make money disappear from the personal accounts of the drug kingpins in Chicago.

The following morning during the meeting they shared the three objectives. Both Johnnie and Lorie said that they wanted to be more involved in the field work. They made a point that once they hacked through the bank firewalls they could take action from anywhere in the world. They did not need to be sitting twiddling their thumbs in the office.

Lorie added that they could also handle getting into the personal accounts and did not need to involve her father or Kekoa both of whom had repeatedly said they were not going to get involved in the drug trade.

Linda nodded and said that was true and that she had no objections to having the two of them participate out in the field.

Johnnie added that he still had Gunjfor and she would be useful in scoping out the various locations that trucks were being loaded. He smiled and said that she would be able to land on the top of the truck and put on a tracking tag so they could easily follow the truck to a point where they could have it stopped and inspected.

Trey suggested that they get a comfortable van that would hold all of them and was modified so they could work from it as they moved about.

Alex was pleased with where the team was coming out. She said that she knew who she was going to get the van from.

They would all work together and operate as often as necessary from their mobile office. She added that if they were on the road with the intention of stopping and inspecting a truck she would need to get the authority to do so and she would want to have Cathy with her.

That same day she put in a call to her father's friend, Rupert, who had provided the conversion bus that she had purchased for the Sins of the Daughter case. He was pleased to hear from her and said that he would create a work of art for her. She said she would come out to see it as soon as he let her know when it was ready. She had only specified that it be bullet proof and that it would comfortably hold six in the back.

She then called Harold and asked him if he was willing to let Cathy work with her team. She was pleased to hear him say that Cathy would be available at her request but she came with the team member that was her partner. He added that the two were a pair and that she knew Lenard, Cathy's partner.

Alex said that she remembered Lennard well because he had been the one who had first greeted her when she had come off the lake after putting the coal barge on fire.

She asked if Lennard was available to meet with her so that Cathy could be introduced to the team.

Harold chuckled and said that Lennard loved pizza and had commented several times that her mother's pizzeria made the best pizza's. He reminded her that Lennard was a shy guy, but she had seen him in action and should know that he was fearless.

2 Finding the Trail

Alex asked if he and Cathy could come to the office for lunch the next day and the spread would feature everything from her mother's pizzeria. That would give all of them a chance to talk over how they could work together.

Harold chuckled and added that if he were included then there was no doubt that Cathy would be available to meet.

3 Field Preparation

My mother always plans ahead. She told me that when she runs on her tread mill she envisions how a case or a situation will unfold. She would run through multiple scenarios and then take concrete actions that would handle all the scenarios that she envisioned. She had envisioned the use of drones and had the entire Cincinnati detective team trained to utilize drones to monitor but also to shoot with. In the case that the team referred to as the Sins of the Daughter she had envisioned having an armored bus with an observation platform from which to fly the drones and she had foreseen the need for motorcycles to chase an adversary through the woods. In that case she had hired a friend of her fathers who specialized in converting buses into what he considered master pieces. She also arranged for the Royal Canadian Mounted Police and the FBI to pay for the bus after convincing them that it would be a cost savings. I learned recently that the bus is still in use by the RCMP.

For her new case, my mother foresaw the need for a large bullet proof van that the team could use. She went back to the provider of the black bus and asked for another of his master pieces. I learned in my journalism class that I cannot mention the brand of van used without getting permission from the owner or supplier due to copyright and trademark laws so I will only say that she went for the top of the line, large van and it came from Germany. That fact and the fact that she had the van bullet proofed brought the price to close to a two hundred and fifty thousand dollars. Wow!!! the price floored me but as I said earlier, my mother is rich and the first case she solved when she opened her private detective service made her richer.

Anyway, after I got over the shock of learning what she paid for it I later learned that like Cathy the dog who saved her life, the van saved the lives of the team. So, the value was not in the beauty of that van but in the functionality that it delivered. And my admiration of Rupert's ability to create his masterpieces went up dramatically. So, let's get on with learning about that masterpiece because it really was a one of a kind van.

The next day in the morning meeting Alex let everyone know that she was going to go to pick up the van at Rupert's Bus conversion shop. She shared with the team that she had asked him to provide her with a top of the line converted van and that it be bullet proofed.

She added that Trey was going with her and they would bring the van back to the office for all of them to get a chance to see it before she had it parked at the marina in a space that had just been built to house it.

Johnnie chuckled and said given her history with cars and with buses, bullet proofing was a great idea. He said that while she was getting the van he was going to fly Gunjfor around the grounds of the Bahá'í House of Worship across the street. He said that he needed the practice because he was sure that they would be using her on this case.

On the way to Rupert's place of business, Trey asked how much she was going to be paying for the new van.

Alex shook her head and said that she really had no clue. She was sure it would be a sum that would make her faint.

When they arrived, Rupert came out and greeted her. He gave her a hug and said that he felt that he had worked magic for her and hoped she would fall in love with the van as much as he had. He then gave Trey a handshake, commented that he looked as fierce as always and said they should follow him in.

Rupert had the biggest black van that Alex had ever seen parked in his show room. He made the point that there was not another one like it. He walked Alex around the exterior and pointed out the cameras that would provide information about everything on all sides of the van. He then opened the large door that went into the left side of the van. It came out and slid towards the back.

Inside were the chairs and table that would comfortably sit six people. He then took her hand and walked around to the other side and opened the door on that side. He pointed out that entry and exit was the same from either side and the step that came out was to make it easy to climb in.

He then highlighted the positioning of the three seats in the back that curved so that each person had a full comfortable seat around the table that was not round but curved on each side and was flat where it came to the sides and jointed seamlessly with the closed doors.

The table had power plugs that he said were for the computers she had mentioned would be used but the connection to the interior network and the internet were wireless.

Rupert then took her hand and guided her up three steps to a platform so she could see the top of the van. He pointed out the antenna that would connect to any cell tower that was providing wireless communications. He smiled and told her that she had the most sophisticated vehicle on the road.

He led the way back to the side of the van where he then pressed a button. It seemed that part of the ceiling of the van was lowering. It turned out to be a eighteen by thirty inch monitor. He smiled and said that she could watch the Real Housewives of Chicago if she desired but it was intended to be a working screen that any computer in the van could use as a display.

She chuckled and asked if he knew the channel for the Real Drug Lords of Chicago.

Trey got her joke, but it was clear that Rupert had no clue what she was joking about.

Rupert pointed out that the van had its own computer mounted behind the back seating area that could serve all six passengers as well as the two people in the front. All they needed were the keyboards that were located under the table in front of each seat. He pointed out that the key boards for the two people in front were up in a shelf above the front window area.

He then patted the exterior of the van and said that he had used a new technique that reduced the weight of bullet proofing. There was a layer of her favorite material, Kevlar, sandwiched between two pieces of stainless steel that would stop almost all caliber of ammunition. The tinted glass was also bulletproof.

He pointed at the tires and said that they were not bulletproof, but they were reinforced so they would deflate in a controlled manner and the van could continue moving because there was a hard rubber inner portion that was good for more than a hundred miles.

He then had her get into the driver's seat and pointed out that she could adjust the seating to accommodate her petite size. He then pointed to Trey and asked him to get in and see how he would fit behind the steering wheel.

Trey nodded but he first adjusted the seat all the way back and down and then got in. There was very little adjustment that he had to do once in. The seat was a great fit.

He smiled and thanked Rupert for choosing such a comfortable seat. He knew that Rupert lived on compliments.

Rupert then pointed out all the controls available to the driver and the passenger. He made a point that all of the seats could be heated or cooled and the temperature in the van could be adjusted in three zones: front, middle and back. He smiled and said that everyone was going to love his van.

He led the way to the back of the van and opened the two doors and pointed out that he had added shelves to accommodate extra storage. He lifted the bottom of the space to show the spare tire. He added that originally it was to be mounted on the back door, but he just could not ruin the sleek look of the van by mounting it there.

Rupert took her hand and guided her to the front of the van and pointed out that he had signed his masterpiece in gold lettering just below the left front headlight.

He smiled, took a small bow and said that it was his most recent conversion master piece and he was extremely happy that it was for her.

Alex ran her index finger over his signature, smiled, and said that she hoped that his master piece would not cost her as much as the bus had cost.

He then said that the bus he had converted for her was still being used by the Canadian RCMP and he had an ongoing contract with them to keep it in top condition.

He smiled and said that conversion was another one he had done from his heart because it had been for her. And it was now a nice ongoing cash flow that he was enjoying.

Alex remembered well the gleaming black bus that the team had used during the case that they called the Sins of the Daughter. That daughter had been a serial killer that killed more than a hundred young men as well as her own sister and her mother. Those facts stood out as much as the beauty of the bus.

Rupert shook his head and said that with the ten percent he was taking off, it was going to cost less than half the cost of the bus.

Trey laughed and said that he was standing behind her in case she fainted.

Alex knew that when she had commissioned Rupert she was most likely facing a quarter of a million dollar cost for the vehicle. She knew that her request to have it bullet proofed would double the cost of a standard conversion van.

She took in the transformation of the top brand of van. She thought the star emblem was an appropriate one. She knew that Rupert was being fair, and that she was personally very impressed with the way he had arranged everything. She knew when she had called him that she would like what he produced. He had forgotten to mention the blend of color of the interior leather, the wood and the rug that had individual light brown foot mats for each passenger. She knew that the team would spend hours in the van and the comfort alone was worth the cost.

She gave Rupert a hug, thanked him for giving her the ten percent discount and asked if Trey could drive the van away from the lot.

Rupert laughed and said of course, he had wondered why she had brought her protector with her since she knew that he personally was such a loving person. He reached into his pocket and took out a fob and handed it to Trey.

Johnnie had been keeping an eye on the office parking lot. He had been flying Gunjfor for almost two hours. He had modified her slightly so that she could carry a transmitting tag that could be tracked on his computer. He figured that they would want to tag trucks they suspected were carrying large sums of money so they could stop them and inspect them. He had been practicing putting the tags down and then retrieving them. He had kept Gunjfor's gun carrying capability and added the ability to carry, place, and retrieve the transmitter wafer. He was very please with Gunjfor's new capability.

When he saw the black van follow Alex into the parking lot, he flew Gunjfor across the street and placed a tag on the top of the van. He walked over and landed Gunjfor and waited to see if he had successfully placed the transmitter undetected.

It was clear that he had succeeded when Alex asked Trey to show the features of the van to the rest of the team. She said that all of them would get qualified to drive the van.

Laurie laughed and said the she hoped the van had good seat belts because she knew she would need them because Linda was a wild lady behind the wheel, and they would all need to hold on.

Linda laughed and said that at least she would get the van out of the parking lot and wondered if her sister would know how to do so.

Alex asked everyone to get in. She then asked Trey to take them out on the highway and when they returned she would treat them to lunch at the Knolton's Marina Golden Goose Restaurant.

Johnnie ran in and got his computer. He took one of the back seats and plugged his computer in. He also started the van's computer and while they were riding toward the highway, he put his tracking routine into the van's computer and brought the picture of a car going along the route they were traveling up on the drop down screen that was on the side of the table next to the right door. He proudly declared that he was tracking the van as they drove along.

Alex looked at the screen and asked what Johnnie was doing since the van came with a program that showed where it was traveling.

Johnnie smiled and said that he had tagged the van and the tag was sending its signal to his ap and doing basically what the van's program did for the van but his tag that had been place on the top of the van by Gunjfor could be put on any vehicle and that vehicle would show up on his ap as the van was currently showing up.

He made the point that they should imagine following a semi-truck that they had tagged.

Alex smiled as she realized that Johnnie had been working on how to intercept trucks that might be carrying the illegal money that was being transported. She complemented him on the great work and said that he could have an extra desert at lunch.

He smiled and said that he was going to hold out for a tray of her cookies.

Lorie decided she would compete a little with Johnnie. She used the vans computer and connection to the internet to connect to her computer that was back at her desk in the office. She then said that she wanted to show everyone the information that she had compiled on the three top money makers in the Chicago drug scene. She was able to call up the accounts of each of the three and show both their private accounts. She then pulled up accounts that they controlled through dummy companies that they managed. She added that she had tapped into all the car dealerships that Harold had named. She smiled and asked if she could get in on Johnnie's tray of cookies reward scheme.

Alex smiled and said she would put in an order with the cookie maker and said that the two had just earned a seat in the van as well.

The ride was as comfortable as Rupert had said it would be and everyone was commenting what a great work environment they would have when they were on the road.

Marisa smiled and asked if their offices were not adequate or were the snacks not good enough.

Linda shook her head and said they were not comparing the office and the van they were comparing the van and the joys of sitting overnight in a sedan as compared to their current seats.

The ride out on the highway was smooth and everyone continued to comment on the attributes of the van. Everyone agreed that the interior was very quiet even when they were in heavy traffic.

Trey commented that it handled like any normal van and did not feel like the tank that he knew he was driving. He drove into the marina and over to the newly modified boat repair area that had been remodeled to accommodate the van.

Alex pressed the fob she had and the door went up automatically. The interior had new paneling; the floor had been redone to have a golden gravel like surface that had a black pad where the van was to be parked. There was at least three feet of clearance on each side of the van as well as in front and back.

Trey commented that a van that cost a small fortune deserved to be parked in a garage that matched it in grandeur.

Alex laughed and said that the garage looked great but it had cost less than ten percent of the cost of the van.

She got out and led the way into the restaurant for lunch.

3 Field Preparation

4 In the Field

Getting to know about the leaders of the Chicago drug cartels was harder for me to do but I was able to get on line and learn about the various cartels and then ask my mother leading questions that slowly gave me a picture of what she was facing.

I thought it was an impossible task but then I am a mere ten year old. I asked everyone on her team questions and I learned about several of her previous cases where she had battled the Gulf Cartel. She had battled the Cartel from an East Coast distributor leader all the way to the top leader in Mexico. I am not sure of the total number of Gulf Cartel members she killed on her first interaction with them but it was something like fifteen including the very top leader in Mexico.

What was really amazing to me was that it was the Gulf Cartel that later defended her by eliminating the Chicago Mafia chief and all his enforcers. They effectively eliminated the entire Chicago Mafia at the request of the friend who was the wife of the cartel boss that my mother had killed !!!

The "Angel on the Hill" as the wife became known was forever a friend to my mother because she had married the Gulf Cartel boss so she could eventually kill him as retribution for he having killed her father. It turned out that she could not kill him. She had prayed that he would get killed.

My mother was the one that did that when he tried to shoot her in the back as she walked away from him after telling her that he was letting her get out of his compound. He had lied to get my mother to turn her back. My mother timed her turn and side step as she heard him retrieve his gun. She turned and shot him between the eyes.

His wife showed my mother a way out of the compound and was forever her friend.

Wow, what a story to learn!

I learned the part about my mother later when I learned why my mother was called, "The Black Angel from the North."

When I learned that, I realized that the two Brazilian drug lords that had killed my parents had stood no chance when they tried to kill her.

I am able to share this information because I was able to keep asking Johnnie enough questions that eventually I had most of the picture. I am sure that as I grow up I will learn more about that story.

So now you know that I am getting to be a good investigator in my own right. I ask questions of each of my mother's team members and they have no clue what I am up to.

I am determined to follow the details of this case. I have set up my own investigative team at school that I feel is almost as good at hacking as Laurie but probably not yet as good as Johnnie. That team and I will have some of the best reports to turn in about the Chicago area social fabric and about the drug scene. We are all getting A's on our reports.

What I found interesting was that the Chicago Cartel bosses all viewed their lives similarly to how "normal" people viewed their lives. Initially I thought that bad people would look in the mirror and realize that they were bad. What I now believe is that each of us see what we wish to see in the mirror. We really don't think about the good, the bad or the ugly. Well maybe the ugly. I wonder if I will ever be as good looking as my mother. And the bad, well I guess I wouldn't think about that so why should those drug bosses?

Well, let me refocus on the case and the fact that my mother, with the help of Johnnie and Laurie was able to get a comprehensive picture of the life and habits of all four drug bosses that she was to deal with. It was at this point in the case that I got to meet the "Angel on the Hill," her brother and his wife. It was interesting to find that very good people often got inextricably tangled up with those in the drug trade. The Angel on the Hill used her connection to help the needy and she and my mother had a common organization in the US. This taught me that even those that were on the other side were often trying to also do good deeds.

*   *   *   *   *   *   *

4 In the Field

Max sat in his luxurious office looking at the pictures of his hometown of Culiacán Rosales, in the state of Sinaloa in Mexico. He missed the social life that he had enjoyed there. His parents both still lived there in the house that he had grown up in. He figured it was time to give them a visit.

The assignment to Chicago had been a reward for his successful management of the flow of cocaine, heroin, and methamphetamine, into the US. He had played a key role in coordinating multi-ton shipments from Central and South America through Mexico into the US. He had used every means to push the drugs into the US. His use of a Boeing 747 cargo aircraft, the implementation of Narco-Subs, the utilization of container ships, use of sleek luxury speed boats, fishing vessels, buses, railcars, tractor trailers and even automobiles to flood the US border from the Gulf coast to the length of the California coast was so successfully that he was promoted.

Now he enjoyed the good life and did not face the continuous gun battles that went on between the cartels. In Chicago money was the weapon of choice. He oversaw a network of strategically placed bribes that kept his drug distributors successfully collecting more money than he could launder. He was constantly bundling the excess and sending it back to Mexico. He was using what he had learned when he had sent drugs into the US to send the valuable US dollar back into Mexico.

He had couriers that he used regularly to fly to various cities in Mexico where they were legitimately going to visit family but in the process they would transport between one to two hundred thousand dollars on their carryon luggage or often on their person. He had enough of them that only about five percent ever got caught. He smiled at the pittance that was lost but the huge effort the authorities used to get that amount.

He had trucks that carried legitimate goods in which more significant sums of money in the range of five to fifteen million dollars were carefully hidden and made their way back to Mexico.

He also had hundreds of across the border couriers that either drove or walked across the border transporting amounts that ranged from one hundred thousand to several million. Again, he flooded the border with them and lost an insignificant amount.

He was now thinking about what his informant at the Police Department Central Headquarters had let him know. A special agent had been assigned to deal with the drug issue in Chicago. He thanked her and let her know that a name for that agent would earn her an extra bonus payment.

He laughed at the thought that anyone could impact the use of drugs in Chicago. He had trouble keeping up with the demand. His biggest problem was the excess cash that he ended up with each month. He figured that he might use some of the extra cash to influence the special agent.

Max looked at his intelligence report that focused on the other two major competitors that he faced. He was familiar with Jose Alfredo of the Jalisco Cartel and Ángel Mayo of the Los Zetas Cartel. He had even faced them in several gun battles. Their behavior was like an open book to him.

The Gulf Cartel leader, Juan Ezequiel-Morales was the one that puzzled him because it seemed that for some reason he had recently greatly decreased that Cartel's distribution presence. He wondered what he knew that he and the other two did not.

A few miles away not far from Max's office, Jose, of the Jalisco Cartel, was sitting in a similar office but he had a view of the waterfront. He had a lease on the top floor of the building he was in and enjoyed the view of the recreation area along the lake waterfront. He often went out along the walk that stretched along the lake front. When he did he usually stopped to enjoy a meal in one to the restaurants that lined the avenue. He smiled as he thought about gulping down four or five Tacos at El Camparina's Tacos before returning to the office. On those days he often ended up needing to take an antiacid to sooth his upset stomach.

Life in Chicago was a relief from the constant gun fights he had been involved in between the Jalisco Cartel and the other cartels that were also present in Chicago. He felt that getting promoted and getting the lush assignment in one of the top drug distribution centers in the US, only New York City was bigger, had been a change that he hoped would last.

The other cartels were all operating in Chicago but at least the battle was not carried out in gun fights but over who could out bribe the various legal organizations so they could operate freely in the areas that they controlled.

He also liked that his primary focus was to manage the cash flow so that it would remain active and continue to grow. His focus had been on growing the number of customers in the area he already controlled. He was successfully investing in real estate and the construction of new buildings. It was a great way to launder money and then invest it in legitimate businesses.

Even so, he often ended up with more money than he could launder in that manner. He had set up a laundering operation in Canada and what didn't get absorbed there he had flowing to Bangkok.

He had the normal management issues that needed handling, but he had farmed that out to his leadership team and periodically met with them to handle any thorny issues.

It was great to be able to relax and enjoy living the good life.

Ángel of the Los Zetas Cartel had assumed a low profile life and spent most of his time on a sixty foot yacht that he often took out fishing. He operated a legitimate grocery goods distribution business. Drugs never entered any of those warehouses.

The trucks bringing in the fruits and vegetables from California, Mexico, and Florida all carried a significant quantity of drugs, but the trucks had an intermediate stop to off load the drugs before arriving at the grocery distribution center.

The trucks would leave Chicago with a variety of locally produced, farm products like corn, wheat and other grains and head back toward Mexico and California. They often transported the excess cash generated by his business. He couldn't think of a better business model than the one he was operating. Drugs came in, got distributed, cash came in from the small drug distributors, it was bundled and then it was going out.

He also had a local money laundering operation using a half dozen used car dealers that dealt strictly in cash. Dirty money went to them; they put it in their bank as sales money. Then periodically sent it to an account that was totally focused on legitimate stock market investments where it made more money. He chuckled as he thought about how easy it was to operate his business.

It was great to be able to relax and enjoy living the good life.

Juan sat in his meeting room with his enforcement team discussing the order that had come to him from headquarters for them to assume a low profile for the coming year or so. He was puzzled by the order and asked if anyone had any idea why they had received the order. He was surprised that the lone remaining enforcer that he had inherited from his predecessor, Ricardo Alverez, laughed and said that he had a good idea.

Ricardo said that there was a new player in the field that had friends in Mexico. This person had earned the protection of the Gulf Cartel several years ago by helping the wife of Ernesto Caldero the Gulf Cartel leader at the time.

To this day the Cartel listened to her, and it was rumored that the person who had just been appointed to reduce the drug flow into Chicago was that friend.

He then shared the fact that he personally had been a participant of a hit on the Mafia boss and his enforcers when they had tried to kill this friend. He had gone in with the rest of the enforcer team and eliminated the entire Mafia operation on behalf of Ernesto's wife. She was now known as the "Angel on the Hill" in the state of Tamaulipas where Ernesto had looked down into Ciudad Victoria and from where he had directed the Gulf Cartel.

Juan asked who this person might be so he would make sure not to kill him.

Ricardo chuckled and said that it was not a he but a petite black woman that had killed more people than anyone he knew including many that had been in the Gulf Cartel that had tried to kill her. He asked if anyone sitting in the meeting had read about or seen the news report on the coal barge that had mysteriously caught on fire and sank in sight of the Chicago waterfront.

Juan nodded and said that he had seen video footage of the barge on fire.

Ricardo smiled and said that was caused by this petite black woman that had gone fishing with her fishing partner on a small fishing boat, but the outing ended with her killing seven armed men and downing a helicopter gunship owned by the Gulf Cartel.

He chuckled and said that she had gone into the fight with only a fishing pole with which to defend herself but it all ended up in a glorious barge fire and seven dead gunmen.

Juan nodded and said that he might enjoy watching what she would do to his three top competitors who might not give her the respect that he was being advised to give. He then said that he was giving them orders to reduce the inflow of drugs and to concentrate on moving the customers out of the district they controlled. He hoped that such action would allow him to keep control of his territory while adhering to the directive coming from the Mexican cartel leader.

Back in the offices of Evercrest, McGregor, Smith and Obrien Partners, Johnnie and Laurie had been able to get through all the firewalls they encountered and were able to set up the cash flow monitoring routines. In only a few days they were able to identify the various accounts used to move money. It was clear to them that most of the accounts they could see did not yield the amounts that they were certain was being accumulated by the drug trade. That difference had to be going out on trucks returning to Mexico.

The only anomaly they detected was that the cash flow for the leader of the Gulf Cartel had greatly reduced in the last few weeks. They shared that with Alex.

Alex smiled and wondered if the "Angel on the Hill" was at work on her behalf. She decided to invite her for a fishing trip on the Golden Goose. The two of them were partners in the charities they both ran and it was time to review their accomplishments and to actually enjoy fishing together.

She asked Marisa to make the invite based on the Golden Goose's and Angelica's availability.

5 Reconnaissance and Observation

I am learning more about the routine used by my mother's team than I had expected. It was interesting to listen to them chat about their drive by observations of the dozens of warehouses that were in use as locations to unload drugs. How they found those warehouses was also interesting. It turned out that Harold and his DEA team had done a lot of the detailed identification of what warehouses were being used by the cartels by tracking the destination of suspected drug carrying trucks. These were trucks identified at the Mexico, US border and tracked to Chicago by participating drug enforcement agencies and inspection stations.

I will confess that I took the opportunity to utilize some of the money I made by being a deck hand on the Golden Goose and working in the bait house to make a few purchases that I utilized to carry out my own devious monitoring of the teams actions. I abided by the rule to put fifty percent of my earnings into my "go to college" bank account. However, I invested in some equipment that I purchased on the internet that allowed me to listen in on what was going on in the team van.

And WOW! There was a lot of dull chatting as I expected but I was able to get the inside scoop on the gun battle in one of the warehouse districts where a car came along side of the van and fired on the van with machine guns.

I could hear Johnnie curse, then the side door open and him talking to Gunjfor, his drone, telling her to get them. I was able to hear Lorie shouting encouragement and then I could hear a crash and Linda saying that Gunjfor got the driver. There was more shooting and the announcement that Johnnie got a second shooter and that the third person had run around the building located on the corner as he was chased by Lorie's drone. I must have listened to that recording at least a dozen times. It was like a scene out of a crime movie only I had to imagine it.

I figure that the seventy five dollars I had spent on that listening device was well spent. I wondered if I could put a small camera on Gunjfor with which I could retrieve both sound and pictures. I decided that I did not want to take the risk of being discovered by Johnnie. He took care of Gunjfor like it was his baby. I also thought about tapping into the camera system that the van had but again I figured I was not good enough to escape being found out by both Johnnie and Lorie.

I was curious how badly the van had been hit but when I went to the garage at the marina where it was parked it was not there.

The next time I saw it I walked around it trying to see where it had been hit but I couldn't find any indication of it having been in a gun battle. I figured that the van had gone back to Rupert who had worked his magic on it.

The other thing I did was to keep track of the vans odometer. I was usually either on the Golden Goose, the bait shop or sometimes at the restaurant when Trey parked the van and then walked back to his office. I would go to the garage and get the reading and put it in my log book. It was interesting to know that almost every day the team put more than two hundred miles on the odometer. There were several times when it exceeded five hundred miles. I correlated my notes to those longer periods and discovered by listening to the team conversation that they were following trucks and identifying the truck stops and logging where they stopped on the way out of Chicago.

It was in this way that I learned they planned to do a surprise inspection and use Cathy the money sniffing dog to find the cash that they suspected was being hauled by a specific truck. I also learned they were not counting on luck but were correlating the movement of money with the cycle that each cartel had of money collection from their street distributors.

I smiled when I thought how thorough and strategic my mother and her team were.

I was personally learning so much on how to be a good observer and I was applying it to everyone at school. I learned who the naturally friendly kids were, who the docile and pushed around kids were and who the bullies were.

My mother had enrolled me in a Tae Kwando class that she and I attended together. I learned that she was a fifth degree black belt. I in short order worked my way up to be a green belt.

I knew that I did not need to worry about any bullies. The school year had only been going on for a couple of months when one of the bully girls confronted me and told me to stay away from her boyfriend. I had no idea who she might be talking about and when she went to push me I grabbed her hand and applied a simple move that had her down on her knees asking me not to break her wrist. I quietly told her to leave me alone then I let go. She jumped up and was going to punch me. This was when I deflected her punch and hit her on the side of her head causing her to stagger back. I looked at her and said that it would only get worse if she continued. She threatened to see me after school but that never happened. To this day, I am a left alone by all the bullies.

But I am supposed to be sharing my learnings about what my mother's team was doing and what they were doing was the observation and reconnaissance in preparation for taking action against all of the major cartels operating in Chicago. The actions were about to net them millions of dollars.

*   *   *   *   *   *   *

Trey had taken on the role as primary driver of the van.

Each morning, he joined the rest of the team on the bike ride into work but he rode on to the marina and put his bike in the parking lot bike rack, went into the garage where the van was parked and drove it back to the office to pick up the team.

Usually, they would all change into some comfortable clothes and hit the restroom before going out to the van. They usually had breakfast at one of several mom and pop places that they had identified served a good breakfast and had a good cup of coffee. Most of them were oatmeal or over easy egg and sausage breakfast eaters. He and Alex often just split a bear claw or a blue berry muffin. They were the lite eaters. He quickly identified Johnnie as the big breakfast eater which was funny because he was also the skinniest of them all.

Alex was very pleased with how the van was working out. She and the team were spending at least thirty hours a week and several times much longer than that riding around getting the proverbial "lay of the land."

Thanks to the information that Harold shared about warehouse locations and the routes that incoming and outgoing trucks took, she and the team were able to get an idea very quickly of what they would be facing once they took the next step to stop and inspect out going trucks suspected of carrying cash.

Johnnie had perfected his ability to use Gunjfor to place and retrieve the tracking chips. He was proud of the ability to swoop in and place the chip on the selected truck and later retrieve the chip when the truck stopped.

He lost only one chip when a truck left the warehouse area and hit every light green and then went down the highway and did not stop at any of the main gas stations. After following that truck for close to one hundred miles Alex called off the chase.

Lorie was trying to get her flying skills to match Johnnie. She had ordered Gunjfor's sister drone. It was a newer model that had the same ability to use a weapon but the weapon was permanently mounted and was lighter which gave her model a longer range and more rounds for her gun. The additional feature was that it had a small reel that allowed it to hover while it picked up an object on a thin woven wire that could lift up to twenty pounds. She had been kidded by the team that she didn't need her drone to pick up her big Mac order. She ended up calling her drone "Gun-for-hire" which did not get the reaction that she had hoped for so she decided instead to name it "Maui" the island that she liked the most. She had spent hours at the target range but was still having trouble getting as good as Johnnie at hitting the target.

Trey had spent hours driving through the various warehouse districts.

He often stopped to let both Johnnie and Lorie fly their drones over the warehouses and observe the unloading and loading processes of the various trucks.

The whole team including the two front seat passengers could see what the drones were seeing. It was as close to being on the dock as they could get.

They spent several late evenings where Johnnie took Gunjfor out over the truck lot and looked back into the warehouses and they could see what was going on inside.

It was on one of these flights that they spotted large squares being buried in what they took to be mega bags of shelled corn.

He had let out a low moan as he realized that the team was not prepared to follow that particular truck as it pulled out and drove away into the dark. It was close to midnight and the team was not ready to make their first stop.

He hated to miss such a sure shot but they all agreed that they were not ready. He drove back to the office dropped everyone off and that night took a taxi home.

The next day they returned to another of the warehouses of interest and Johnnie and Lorie were just getting their drones ready when a dark blue sedan slowed down and started to shoot at them with machine guns. It was a total surprise and an unexpected attack.

Trey heard Johnnie curse and then the far side back door opening. He watched as Johnnie expertly flew Gunjfor around the front of the van and shot the driver causing him to drive forward and hit the light post on the other side of the street. The shooter in back jumped out and again fired at the side of the van and was surprised when Gunjfor swooped in and shot him in the forehead. He was dead before he hit the ground.

He then saw Maui swoop out from behind the van and shoot at the third shooter who was running for cover toward the old building on the corner.

He shouted to the two of them to get back in the van. As soon as they were in he drove slowly away from the scene. He heard Alex calling the police chief to let him know what had happened and that they were leaving the scene of the shooting so they would not be outed to the cartel that controlled that area.

He drove back to the office, dropped everyone off and then drove the van directly to Rupert's conversion lot. He parked the van out of sight in the back. He took a taxi back to the marina and finally rode his bike home. The next day the team met at the office to review and analyze what had occurred.

Johnnie made the point that they had over observed and it was time that they took action.

Alex listened to the team and when the meeting reached the point where the talk began to repeat itself, she called an end to the meeting.

She called the chief of police and discussed the situation and if there was anything that they needed to address. The Chief had chuckled and said that it was such a common scene that he and his men had put it down as another inter rivalry gang shooting. Alex let him know that the team was convinced that they had spent too much time observing and were going on to the next phase of their effort to reduce the flow of drugs.

She next called Harold and asked if Lyle and Cathy, the money sniffing phenom, were available on the following day.

Harold asked if he could also be part of the first stop. Alex smiled knowing that it was really his polite way of saying that he was coming along. She chuckled and said that she had the space as long as Cathy was willing to sit on the floor.

She called Rupert and was assured that she would have the van back in immaculate condition by that afternoon but he was quite unhappy about it receiving such brutal treatment.

She then smiled when he asked if she approved of the bullet proofing that he had done. She knew that he was personally pleased at his light weight way of doing the bullet proofing. She replied that not only was she pleased but she was giving him a ten per cent tip for the quick repair service and another five per cent for the having done such good bullet proofing. She heard Rupert laugh and say that he was pleased to be of service.

Late in the afternoon Marisa announced the arrival of the van. The driver greeted all of them when they came out. He pointed to the side of the van and said that the paint was not yet totally set and they should keep their hands off the paint. He added that he had lost count on the number of bullet holes after he passed one hundred.

Trey walked along the side and commented that it was impossible to tell that the side had looked like Swiss cheese when he had left it on the lot and now it looked immaculate and just like new.

A cab pulled into the lot and the driver said that he was returning to his work, and that Rupert had sent his greetings and asked him to let Alex know that he had tipped his very skilled driver twenty percent for the delivery.

Alex laughed and told him to let Rupert know that she thanked him for the speed with which he had done the work.

Trey took the van, parked it in the garage, and walked back to the office and left work by bike with the rest of the team.

They had all agreed to taking action the next day.

6 The Nose in Action

I was concerned about being discovered by someone cleaning the van. I asked my mother if the company would hire me to clean out the van on a weekly basis. I didn't want to seem too eager so I asked for fifty dollars a cleaning knowing that my mother would turn it down.

That got a laugh from my mother who countered with ten dollars a cleaning.

I thought about it and said thirty.

She again laughed and offered fifteen dollars.

I would have settled for fifteen but I shook my head as if I was going to reject that and she then said twenty.

So now once a week I make twenty bucks and feel confident that my spy equipment that I hid under one of the front seats is safe from discovery.

I love the fact that my mother is so much fun to be around.

Let me now get back to reporting what I learned happened not long after the shoot out and the repair of the van.

I could relate the boring details of the days before the first stop was made but let me skip to the day that Cathy the "Nose" had her first success.

The team was following a truck associated with the Jalisco Cartel. My mother had chosen that cartel to be the first to be hit and to be hit repeatedly because that was the cartel that had shot up the van. I can tell you that was the reason because I listened to the team agree to kick that cartel in the butt.

Yeah! That was actually what Johnnie said right after he had used Gunjfor to put a tag on the truck so they wouldn't lose it in traffic. What was really funny was that Cathy barked as if she was agreeing with him. I just laughed when I listened because I thought that the conversation between the team members was usually sort of boring but occasionally one of them seemed to hit the right tone. It was like listening to a concert that was playing a piece that periodically had the large base drum beating a thunderous tone or a flute screeching a high pitch wail that made the audience wake up. If I closed my eyes, I could imagine the team playing a piece by the way they joked and exchanged jabs with each other. In a way it comforted me to know that they seemed so relaxed.

Well anyway, this was a day that Cathy earned the meager reward she was given for finding the bundle of money that was in hidden in one of the two thousand pound bags.

I listened in to the conversation as Trey followed the truck and learned that they were fairly certain that they were following a truck that had a high probability of transporting money but they were going to need a reason to pull it over and get it inspected.

When the truck drove past the exit that led to the truck stop that the team had hoped it would use, I heard Linda suggest that they monitor the speed of the truck to see if they could get the highway patrol to pull it over. Trey commented that the truck was staying a few miles per hour below the speed limit and that would not work.

Then Johnnie said that my mother should shoot out one of the tail lights and then they could call in the highway patrol. I was really surprised when I heard her agree. I could hear the wind when she opened the window on the passenger's side of the van and then a very quiet pop. I was expecting the gun to be louder and I expected that she would take several shots.

Later, out of curiosity I asked Johnnie what it would take to hit something when shooting out of a moving vehicle. He laughed and replied that it took the skill that my mother, who was known on the team as the "Black Annie Oakley" had. I asked him about that and learned that she was known throughout the nation's police departments as the deadliest shot that anyone knew.

I was already taking Tae Kwando classes with her so I decided to ask her about going to the gun range with her and learning to shoot a gun.

Anyway, I was sharing what I had garnered about the stop where Cathy the nose did her job. The highway patrol stopped the van, got the driver out and was showing him the broken tail light when my mother approached the two and showed the patrolmen her Illinois detective license.

She said that she suspected the truck to be carrying drugs. Cathy was brought out and she handed the driver a search warrant.

Cathy and Lyle, her handler were able to get on top of the two thousand pound bags.

Lyle had to crawl along the top and follow her across the large bags of some sort of bagged material that I heard Lorie say smelled like eggs gone bad.

Once Cathy identified one of the pallets as having money in it everyone got back into the van and followed the truck to the truck stop were it was off loaded and Cathy then went around each bag and identified three of the pallets as having money hidden in them.

I listened as Cathy's handler sat on the floor at the side of the van and praised her as he gave her a treat.

From listening to the team, I learned that there indeed were large bags of money hidden in three of the large bags. Lorie was guessing that they had potentially snagged three million dollars.

Later I learned that after the bundles of money had been taken back to the Chicago Police Department been counted it turned out that Lorie had guessed millions of dollars too low.

Cathy had sniffed out close to twelve million dollars and her reward was a few dog treats.

I laughed as I thought how underpaid she was.

I figured that I should bargain a better treat for her.

*   *   *   *   *   *   *

Alex came down to breakfast and found Aurea chatting with her mother who was frying two eggs over easy in butter and spreading a piece of toast with strawberry mango jam for her. She asked if she could have the same as she poured herself a cup of coffee. She was still getting over her anger at the Jalisco Cartel for having machine gunned her team while they were sitting parked in the warehouse district near the Jalisco warehouse that received and sent out semi-trucks. It was an action that only a very vindictive person would take. She figured that she would repay that person by taking as much money away from him as possible.

She was sipping on her coffee when she was surprised by Aurea asking to be hired to regularly clean the van. It was something that she had not even thought about. She knew that Aurea would be practicing her bargaining skill with her as she had with all the jobs she had bargained for, and she always bargained for a high wage. She was pleased that Aurea was earning top dollar at every job she had at the Marina.

She enjoyed bargaining with her daughter and for her it was not about the money as it was about the two of them both enjoying the bargaining. When she asked Aurea how often she would clean the van and how much she wanted for each cleaning she was not surprised that the response was fifty dollars for each cleaning and the frequency was once a week.

She laughed and replied that it was way too much and said she would pay ten dollars for each weekly cleaning and fifteen for any special requested cleaning.

She listened as Aurea came down to thirty with special request cleanings being the same price. She wondered what rate her ever industrious daughter had in mind and offered fifteen.

She watched as Aurea shook her head slightly as if she was going to counteroffer so she offered twenty and said that was as high as she would go.

That got a smile from Aurea.

She then knew that Aurea had won the bargaining.

She went to her and gave her a hug and said that she wanted a good job done every Saturday and that the usual split of money go to into the college fund.

That day at the morning meeting she shared the breakfast scene with the rest of the team.

She was not surprised that Johnnie laughed and said that Aurea had come out on top.

Laurie added that she was sure that they would get into a clean van every Monday and that was worth every penny that Aurea was getting.

Alex nodded and said that she agreed and then asked for a report on what each team member had learned about what went through the warehouses of the four drug cartels.

Linda spoke up first and reported on what was going through the Jalisco warehouses besides the drugs they imported. She stopped and pointed to Johnnie and Lorie and thanked them for giving her access to the product export logs. She then shared the fact that the warehouse ran a legitimate business that imported automobile spare parts made in Mexico and the majority of what they sent back were Illinois grown cash crops of hard wheat, yellow corn, and sorghum.

She smiled and said that she had done some additional learning research on how the cash crops were used. She listed her learning and let the team know that the yellow corn went mostly to feeding pigs and chickens, the white corn was ground into a flour and used to make tortillas; hard wheat was ground into flour, used in breads, tortillas and other baked goods; barley went almost one hundred percent into making beer; soybeans was pressed for its oil, ground into flour for use in tortillas and baked goods; crushed into a meal to feed livestock, also for use in aquaculture and feeding farm raised tilapia. She added that sorghum was another grain that went into making tortillas and bread.

She then highlighted the fact that from her deep dig, sixty percent of the trucks going back to Mexico for the cartel returned with farm products and about forty percent hauled a variety of products such as car parts, electronic goods, and personal care products.

She finished by adding that the drug money that was going periodically back to Mexico would be hidden in one of the products being taken back.

Alex thank Linda for the deep dig and suggested a break.

After the break she asked Johnnie for his report.

Johnnie had done the research on the Sinaloa cartel warehouses and said that he had learned that they ran their business in a very similar way of mixing legitimate with illegitimate business.

He then shared the general mix of goods going back to Mexico. He said that about thirty percent were farm products, forty percent were Electronics of some sort and the surprise for him was that the US sent auto parts into Mexico and it represented thirty percent of what the cartel trucked back. From what he could tell, the cartel liked to ship the money back hidden inside truck gear boxes and inside automatic transmissions. He added that it seemed that each time the cartel randomly used a different way back to Mexico and used a different border crossing point.

Lorie said that she had similar boring statistics but the Los Zetas shipped back more auto parts to the tune of fifty percent. The other fifty percent was equally split between industrial electrical components and farm grains. From what she could make out it seemed that the money would be hidden in the electrical components like power distribution boxes or panels.

Trey spoke up next and said that he had picked up on a sharp decline in the truck shipments of incoming drugs for the Gulf Cartel.

He smiled and said that it seemed that the decline corresponded with Alex being asked to reduce the amount of incoming drugs and he wondered if the reduction was on purpose. He went on to share that the Gulf Cartel was also heavy into sending car parts back to Mexico. It represented forty percent of what went back. Transporting barrels of oil back represented fifty percent of the truck volume. The final ten percent was made up of computer equipment and personal care products.

From what he could figure out the money going back to Mexico went either submerged in oil barrels, in bags of dog food or in personal care products like shaving cream cans. He shook his head and said that the cartel had effectively Cathy proofed their shipments.

Alex then shared that the DEA had arranged an inspection area at the first stop most often used by trucks leaving from the Jalisco warehouse. The team would follow the next truck they suspected was transporting cash and when it stopped they would serve the warrant allowing them to inspect the truck and get Cathy in position to do her job. If she indicated a positive hit the truck would be off loaded and a detailed search would be performed.

Linda nodded and said that the next money truck would likely be leaving the next morning.

Alex suggested they all get to bed early because the van would leave the parking lot at three in the morning. She had arranged for Lyle to bring Cathy and join them when they arrived at the warehouse to tag the semi that would likely be carrying the money.

It was a little past three thirty in the morning when Johnnie flew Gunjfor down the block to the warehouse area, located the van being loaded and planted the tracking transmitter on its top.

After Lyle and Cathy were dropped off and got into the van Trey drove to the gas station located at the entrance of the interstate where they would wait for the truck.

Marisa had prepared a breakfast box for them that had an egg, sausage sandwich and either a donut or for Alex one half of a bear claw. Each of them had a thermos of coffee that fit in the cup holder by each of their chairs. They sat quietly chatting about what they hoped would happen and if they were successful how fast they might be able to have an impact on all the cartels.

Johnnie had been monitoring the movement of the truck and let Trey know that the truck was a block away.

Trey thanked him and prepared to follow.

Three hours later they passed the exit where they had expected the truck to make its first stop.

Linda asked if they could get the highway patrol to stop the truck for speeding.

Trey shook his head and said that the driver had stayed at or below the speed limit for the entire time.

Johnnie suggested that they get the highway patrol to stop the truck for a broken tail light.

Linda said that it didn't have a broken tail light.

He laughed and said that the breaker was sitting in the front seat.

Alex smiled and said that she agreed that a broken tail light would be the way to get the truck stopped. She opened her window, asked Trey to pull out and pass the truck and then aimed her Glock and fired. The main right tail light shattered and Trey sped forward and passed the truck.

Alex called in the Highway patrol and asked that they pull the truck over. A few minutes later a highway patrol car approached and pulled the truck over.

Alex approached the two patrol officers that had the driver at the back of the semi showing him the broken light as they wrote up a ticket. She thanked them, showed the paper work authorizing her to search the semi.

Lyle brought Cathy to the truck. He and Trey lifted her up and got her on top of the large super bags that the semi was carrying.

The odor was a little overwhelming and Alex was worried that it would hinder Cathy's ability to smell the money. She had just about given up hope when Cathy barked indicating a hit.

Alex then let the two Highway patrol officers know that they were taking the truck back to the truck stop where a DEA team was waiting to off load the truck and do a more thorough inspection of what might be hidden in the super bags.

Lyle showed the two his paperwork authorizing him to drive the semi back and asked them to take the driver back with them. He got into the truck and was surprised when Alex got into the passenger's side, smiled, and asked if she could ride along.

He had Cathy scoot over nearer to him and asked Alex to put on her seat belt.

Once back at the truck stop, the DEA team took over. They off loaded four super bags resting on huge pallets. Lyle led Cathy over and in rapid order she indicated that the three super bags that had been toward the front of the semi all had money hidden in them. The bags turned out to contain sorghum and each bag had three rectangular hay bale sized heavy plastic sealed squares filed with money. The bales were loaded into a waiting van and sent off to get opened and counted. The driver was cuffed and put into a second DEA van to be taken to a detainment center to be charged with smuggling.

Alex and team got back into their van. It was nearing dinner time so she asked what the team wanted to do.

Trey, Johnnie, and Lyle said they were planning to go home. Linda and Lorie said that they would eat at the Golden Goose and then go back to their apartment.

Alex said she would go home and that they should all plan on meeting at ten the following day so they could plan their next hit.

7 Disruption Reaction

*B*y listening to the conversations of my mother and her team as they repeatedly stopped the trucks suspected of carrying the drug money back to Mexico I learned that they were being exceptionally effective. They were actually causing the cartels severe economic pain. And it was a pain that I learned was causing the Cartel bosses to consider working together.

I learned that Johnnie was able to intercept messages that pointed to the fact that the Jalisco, the Sinaloa, and the Los Zetas cartels had lost more than fifty million dollars each. I heard them talking about the fact that the Chicago Gulf Cartel organization was the exception and was maintaining its presence by allowing the distributors for the other cartels to service their clients as they greatly decreased the flow of their own drugs into Chicago. That meant that they were not sending any money from Chicago to Mexico and were effectively sitting on the sideline.

This was a surprise to me, though the teams seemed to think that it was in line with what they knew about that Cartel.

I also learned that the DEA had let the team know that the Gulf Cartel distribution outside of Chicago had actually increased. So, it verified what I had learned about the cartel choosing not to confront my mother's team.

Wow! Now that is what I took as making an impression and I thought how smart that was of the Gulf Cartel leaders. They were letting the other cartels take the hit.

I heard my mother say she was sending a message to the "Angel on the Hill" to have her thank the Gulf cartel leaders for their consideration. She told the team that this meant that at least for the short term the Gulf Cartel was making their job easier. I heard her add that none of them should believe that the Cartel had any intentions of reducing their drug flow into the US.

I listened as Trey replied that the drug trade was like an amoeba, when law enforcement pushed on one side it retracted but bulged out on the other side.

He made the point that they were having an imaginary impact on the Chicago drug trade and in reality what they were doing was putting the cartels' Chicago money into the DEA's bank account but the cartels would bounce back because the demand would remain and the shortage of drugs meant that the users would pay more and the amoeba would once again maintained its overall shape.

I agreed with Johnnie when he pointed out that the only really effective action would be to figure out how to reduce the number of people desiring to buy the drugs.

He added that another approach would be to legalize drug use and put a tax on the drugs that would pay for the harm that it did to the people in the long run.

I figured that the political solution would never happen in my life time.

Just imagine how I was affected as I lay in bed late at night listening to what had happened during that day. It was like watching a crime thriller in my head.

Only it was real!

I was sure that I was getting addicted to the action.

What I found fascinating was how the team worked at anticipating what each cartel would do.

My mother was always one that followed the Boy Scout motto of "Be Prepared." She had the team practicing with their individual armed drones.

I learned that she was the only one that could fly simply by monitoring the coordinates on her display. This meant that she could remain hidden and still attack a specific target and effectively fire the weapon that her drone carried.

I felt better knowing that when she was in a gun battle she would be able to remain behind cover.

I now laugh at myself because later while I listened in on the team conversation I learned that she was the one that ran into the line of fire as she was flying her drone and dodging gunfire so she could get into position to where she could do more damage.

It turns out I was naïve in thinking that she would get behind shelter and fight from there.

She ran towards that shooters! She was the person who attacked the attacker!

The thought that she ran towards the shooters has stayed in my head for days. I heard Lorie comment that someday she wanted to be as brave as her "Aunt," my mother.

Wow!, Wow!, Wow!

Now my time with her at Tae Kwando and the gun range meant so much more.

I was practicing with, my mother, a heroine !!!

I focused my efforts at getting better. I earned my black belt in Tae Kwando.

At the firing range, I was able to hit the bullseye with an entire round of my gun.

At school I was working on having the best grade in the class but there was a set of twins that were a smidge better. I learned that there would always be someone better than me. But I was focused on getting a little better every day.

I was also determined to be prepared.

I wanted to be as brave and prepared as my mother.

My gosh I almost forgot to share what my mother did to be prepared. Yes I mentioned the drones, but my mother had purchased a new drone for everyone. These drones were in addition to the drones each of the team already had.

She had ordered specially modified drones that featured a nine millimeter caliber, four inch button riffled gun tube that carried one hundred rounds of nine millimeter bullets. The weapon was similar to a Glock 19 except it was a drone.

Additionally, it had two high powered lights and a high volume loudspeaker. If the lights and speaker were not used the drone had a forty-five minute flight time.

She even got one for me but mine did not have the weaponry on it, but I did learn to fly it with the rest of the team.

And flying with them was like flying with the famous World War Two, Red Tails flying squadron. I am sure that was what my mother had in her mind because each of the barrels on the drones were painted red.

Watching the practice that my mother made them go through and how accurate they became with their flying weapons made me feel much better about them getting in a fight with the cartels. I watched as each of them learned to hit a target on the ground from a drone that was barely visible in the sky.

In their final practice flight that I watched they flew in formation toward a set of targets and together took out all five targets. It was such a great way for them to end practice.

I want to step back a little from all the talk about weapons and share that my mother had the crime fighting side where she was deadly, and she had the passionate side where she focused on helping those in need.

So, I want to share the fact that I have also embraced the side where she embraces the concept of, "Doing a good turn daily" and "Treating others as you wish to be treated." I have visited her Helping Hands farm in Ohio and know that she runs that to help young women and has recently expanded the program to take in young men that need help in getting their lives back on track, and to take up living a productive fear free life.

So, I am personally not short of stretching goals or in need of any additional role models to emulate. I have my mother who gives both to me and her team that expands that to the horizon.

But let me refocus on sharing the fact that the team was expecting to face some serious retribution from the cartels. It made me worry about each of them and it made me see them in a new light. They were all heroes or heroines in my eyes. It also made me make sure that I did the best job I could at keeping the bullet proof black van spotless.

That was the least that I could do to help!

* * * * * * *

Alex ordered the newest brand of drones that she had specially modified to be more deadly. The drones featured a nine millimeter caliber four inch button riffled gun tube and carried one hundred rounds of nine millimeter bullets mounted on a compact gimbal that let the gun barrel rotate three hundred and sixty degrees. The weapon was similar to a Glock 19.

Additionally, the drone had two high power lights and a high volume loudspeaker. If the lights and speaker were not used the drone had a forty-five minute flight time. She hoped not to be in a gun battle that lasted that long.

She asked Trey to use his combat experience and design the practice that they would hold. She stipulated that she wanted everyone to hit what the camera on the drone was seeing and to be able to do so from the maximum rated distance of the drone's weapon.

Trey shared that they would do their target practice out on the lake where they could do so and not be at risk of having stray bullets harm anyone. He added that they first needed to learn to fly their drones and not be worried about crashing them into the water. He picked a local park where they could hold ammunition free flights. He had Matt melt some lead into blocks equivalent in weight to the ammunition each drone would carry. Once the drones were ready, he led the flight training phase until everyone could launch and land their drones smoothly.

He arranged with Matt to take them out on the Golden Goose for three days of target practice. The practice consisted of launching the fully armed drones and then firing on five floating targets. He then set the qualification criteria that they hit the bullseye on the target ten times on their qualifying flight.

Alex took her drone up and got the feel of it by swooping in on her target and then flying away. She did this serval times to get the feel of the conditions out on the lake.

The wind was a little stronger than it had been in the park. She shot several test shots to see where her bullet would land. Once she had her eye synchronized with the view on the camera she took her shots and about every other shot hit the bullseye. By the time she had shot fifty rounds she had twenty five holes in the bullseye. She then rapid fired the remainder of her ammunition and literally pulverized her target.

She turned, pumped her hand in the air, and asked Trey if she had qualified. She smiled when he declared her the "Annie Oakley of Lake Michigan."

Trey qualified on his second flight.

Johnnie was the next to be able to qualify on his fourth flight.

Linda and Lorie laughed as they went up on their seventh flight on the second day out. That was the flight when they each qualified. They both commented that they had come into the flight competition thinking they were pretty good, but they were humbled by the old folks on the team.

Johnnie brushed back his almost white curly head of hair, laughed and said that everyone on the team seemed really quite young to him.

Alex said that on the following day they would all fly at the same time and synchronize their attack on the different targets in the formation that Matt called out to them.

The following day Matt had the team swooping, swerving, and flying in coordinated attacks on the targets below. A few close calls occurred but none of the drones dropped out of the sky.

Trey announced that all of the team should be considered flying drone magicians.

Back in the City, Juan was taking stock in what had been happening and was listening to his team report about the raids that were taking place and making a significant negative impact on his competitors.

He realized that the directive from the Mexican headquarters to reduce the flow of drugs to Chicago and to focus on keeping the legitimate businesses making money had been exactly the right advice.

He also learned that the other three cartels were planning a joint hit when the next truck was stopped. They planned to put gunmen in the trailer that they figured would be stopped and to also have a squad of riflemen positioned at the end of the truck lot where the truck would be pulled to get off loaded to have its cargo inspected.

He contacted his boss and asked what the Gulf Cartel should do. The direction that he was given surprised him. He was to take the opportunity and help the "Black Angel of the North" and send as many of the other cartel gunmen to meet their maker as he could. It was an opportunity that the Gulf Cartel should use to get more control in Chicago.

He decided that one of the actions that he would take was to warn "The Black Angel" about the ambush that the other cartels were planning.

He did not want to take any chances by using the internet, so he sent his message by courier on a piece of paper.

Alex heard a loud knock on the front door of the house. She told everyone to stay where they were and she would be right back. She cautiously approached the door to see who it might be. She knew from past experience that her father had built a door that a twelve-gauge shot gun slug could not penetrate so she was confident as she looked out the peep hole.

She could hear a car driving away. She cautiously opened the door and saw the manila envelope. When she opened it she smiled. The message was simple, and it was very clear to her who had sent the message.

It read, "The Angel on the Hill" sends greetings and has asked me to warn the "Black Angel of the North" about a planned bushwack the next time a truck is pulled into the lot for inspection.

She knew that the message had been sent by Juan Ezequiel-Morales the Chicago Gulf Cartel leader, and she knew that the reduction of the drug distribution that the cartel was currently practicing was due to Angelica's continued influence in the operation of the Gulf Cartel.

She shook her head and went back inside to enjoy sitting by the pool and watching Aurea swim. The cream soda on ice tasted especially sweet.

She got back into the discussion of the latest case where her mother wanted her to help one of her clients.

She knew that she would need to prepare the team the next day.

8 Ambushers, Ambushed

I really felt like the proverbial fly on the wall during this last week. It was one of my scarier weeks. The team was trying to figure out exactly how the cartels might try to get back at the team.

My mother shared the message that had been sent to her. When she read it to the team, she said that she was sure that the message was from the leader of the Chicago Gulf Cartel. She added that she suspected that he might have an ulterior motive for sending the message. She was certain that he had been given the order by the top Mexican Gulf Cartel leader, but he most likely was also making sure that the other three cartels didn't somehow come out on top.

It was interesting to hear how my mother expertly guided the team and got it prepared for a battle with the cartels.

I was to learn later that she intuitively guessed that other than the Gulf Cartel, the other three Chicago cartels were planning a coordinated trap.

She guessed since she had been warned, the next stop of a truck would be the one that was a trap. She added that the trap would be sprung at the inspection location.

I also learned that the location for the next stop was located about two and a half hours west of Chicago at a large truck stop more or less in the middle of nowhere.

My mother said that if the truck they were following drove into that station as if to fill up on gas, it would be a trap. She expected that there would be gunmen inside of the truck and also located in the woods at the back edge of the lot where the DEA had setup to have the truck inspected.

I laughed when I heard her say that she had a special gift for Cathy and it turned out to be a Kevlar body vest. She handed Lyle the foot booties that went with the full body vest that even covered Cathy's snout and legs. When he asked why the vest was missing a tail cover I had to sit down because I was laughing so hard.

My mother said that her tail wagged too fast to get hit.

I wish I had been there to see Cathy in her outfit. My mother made everyone wear a full Kevlar outfit including head covers so it made sense to me that she had thought of Cathy.

Later after the fact I learned that the trap set by the three cartels was very close to what my mother had anticipated but the twist that she had not foreseen was that the Gulf Cartel got into the action in the most unexpected way.

The cartel drove a flatbed truck that had been modified so that a half dozen men laying down behind a four inch thick and two foot high barrier could fire high powered rifles between openings.

The morning of the trap, they came through the farm field that surrounded the truck stopped. The other cartels drove three trucks into the lot and parked them so they could shoot everyone.

When my mother held a debriefing after the shootout she shared the fact that the Gulf Cartel had taken the opportunity to make sure they would have the upper hand for the foreseeable near term future by shooting the shooters in the three trailers. She was sure that their drug trade would boom as soon as her assignment ended.

Then I heard Cathy being thanked for her heroic action of crushing the wrist of a gunman that was about to shoot my mother. That was a surprise, and I learned later that my mother was about to get shot when Cathy took a long run, leap and crushed the wrist of a gunman about to shoot my mother.

Now I have a dog heroine that I am going to make sure gets treats from me !!

Alex knew that she had done everything possible to have everyone ready to deal with any reprisal actions that any of the Cartels might decide to try. She highlighted that one of the most likely scenarios was for the cartel to put gunmen in the semi-truck trailer to shoot whoever was opening the doors and then come out shooting.

She added that if the truck they were following drove up into the gas station that the team and the DEA had selected she was sure it would be a trap. She wanted to make sure that the van would park off to one side so they would be out of the direct line of fire. She would make sure that the DEA folks would stand off to the other side behind some sort of barrier that would shield them. She then asked if there were any questions.

Linda asked if they should have their drones ready.

Trey smiled and said he had not practiced for hours to miss out using his drone in a gunfight. He added that if the team flew their drones like they had done in practice the gunmen would be shooting at the drones and not at them. He shook his head and said that he hoped that was what the gunmen would do because then the team might lose a couple of drones but they would face fewer bullets flying their way. He smiled and said that he loved his Kevlar vest but the pain that he had endured the last time he was in a frontal gun battle was more than he wanted to endure again.

Johnnie chuckled and said that as soon as the van stopped and before the back doors of the stopped semi were opened he suggested that they all have their drones up in the air.

Lorie said that she seconded that.

Alex voiced her agreement and suggested that they spread out and lay on the ground while they were flying their drones. She wanted to make sure that they kept a three hundred sixty degree mentality if any gunfire did break out.

She added that she did not want to forget the other trucks in the lot or any other location where more gunmen might be prepositioned.

Maximilian arrived to the late night meeting with a half dozen enforcers. They were in the drive through warehouse situated near Bubbly Creek. One enforcer stayed at the fifty caliber machine gun mounted in the pickup as he waited for the other three cartels leaders to arrive.

The warehouse was currently up for sale and empty. This allowed each Cartel to come in through a different door. He watched as the Jalisco Cartel came in almost equal numbers and a truck with a machine gun of their own. Not long after the Los Zetas duplicated the approach.

He was surprised that the Gulf Cartel, one of the strongest in Chicago only came in with a stretch limo. He figured it was Juan's way of showing his confidence. Maximilian decided that he would later show the ass what power really meant. At the moment he just looked a Juan as he walked casually to the table that had been placed dead center between the four cartels.

Juan took in the scene and from the fact that they were brandishing their fire power he figured they were looking for revenge. He was saving his energy and getting his men into position while the other cartels were paying attention to each other. He asked his three bodyguards to stay at the car as he got ready to walk to the table that had been set up in the middle of the space bracket by the four groups.

8 Ambushers, Ambushed

As he walked causally toward the table he watched the other three leaders do the same. He wondered what they had in mind.

Once they were all sitting at the table, Maximilian took the lead and proposed that they get rid of the group that had cost all of them close to one hundred fifty million dollars. He suggested a three hundred sixty degree ambush from three strategically positioned semi-trailer trucks in the truck lot and with some men in the woods along the backside of the truck lot.

He put a map of the parking lot down and put three x's down to indicate where the trucks would be parked and another x in the woods. He put a circle around the center location of the three truck x's to indicate where the truck to be inspected would be parked. He then asked which location each of them wanted to take.

Juan decided to let the other cartels chose first. He wanted to make sure that his men would be in a good position but he did not want to show his hand. The other two cartels chose the other two truck x's which left him with exactly the spot he had wanted.

He would be located almost directly opposite of the other three cartels.

It would give his men the ability to shoot any of the other cartel's gunmen in an almost undetectable way. He wanted to laugh but he kept a poker face.

Each cartel was to put three men into the truck to be inspected. His three men in that truck would be at the most risk. He wondered what he could do to protect them. All he could think of was to tell them to stay to the back and to lay down on the bed of the truck and wait until the shooting was over and to give themselves up. He hated to put them into that situation, but he could not think of any other way that would not expose his hand.

At about the same time, Harold was coaching his DEA team about the stop that would take place the following morning. He shared that Alex had suggested having two rock filled dumpsters placed to the side of the spot where the semi would be parked for offloading where they could take cover.

She added that he should only have one person open the back door but standing at the side using a rope to pull it open and make sure to step to the side and get away from the van as they were doing it.

He shook his head and said that he would do it himself because he didn't want to put anyone into that situation. He added that he was going to get a small dumpster put to the side, so he had something to hide behind once he opened the door.

He reminded everyone that it was to be a full Kevlar suit day to include gloves, sox, and head gear. He added that they were to wear their DEA hats and DEA jackets.

Lyle led Cathy in wearing her full Kevlar outfit and said that it was a gift from Alex. She had instructed him to make sure that Cathy did not get hurt so she could continue doing her outstanding job at sniffing out the money.

Everyone in the meeting laughed and gave Cathy a pat as she walked by. He added that Alex had also suggest being in full body suits.

As the meeting in the warehouse came to a close, Maximilian said that he was looking forwards to wiping out the bitch that had cost he and his organization so much of a loss and had disrupted the flow of drugs coming up from Mexico. All the cartels voiced their agreement and Juan joined in.

He had not felt the sting that the other cartels had because he had focused on optimizing the legitimate businesses and moving the distribution of the drugs to the cartel markets that could use it. In fact, he had been thanked by a couple of his cartel friends for helping them out.

He was instead thinking about how he wanted the outcome of the ambush to be. He planned to do his part as directed by headquarters and he hoped that his warning to Alex would allow that team to survive. As he looked at the three trucks with the machine guns he knew that the overwhelming fire power would most likely rest with the three cartels in the truck.

In the morning, a day later, he wished his three members that would be in the truck to be stopped good luck.

One of them pointed to their yellow shoes, their yellow hats and said to let the rest of the team know that they would have them on and not to shoot them. The three were assured that no one was going to shoot them but they should stay to the back and stay low.

As the gunmen were getting into the trailer, and Gunjfor was placing the tracking tag on top of the truck, Johnnie recognized the fifty caliber being bolted to the truck bed.

Once again the memory that was now close to fifty years old of him feeling the pulsing of the fifty as he dished out death swept over him.

It almost caused him to lose control of Gunjfor.

When he was putting her away, he let the team know that it was the day they had been practicing for and to get their drones loaded.

He showed them the view of the gunmen getting into the van and the fifty being bolted to the deck. There were two pallets loaded chest high that would serve as protection for those standing behind them but what was really frightening was the fifty caliber machine gun and its large ammo box with the bandelier going up to the weapon.

He made the point that to him that gun was the gun of death.

Trey nodded and said that they should expect more than just the gunmen that would be in that truck. If he were setting the attack scene, he would use the truck they were stopping as the bait for a bigger attack.

He said that they should look for anything out of the ordinary when they pulled into the truck stop. He added that they needed to make sure they were not in the sites of any fifty.

Alex reminded them that if the truck went up into the truck stop on its own it was clear that the driver wanted to be stopped and get moved into the inspection, unload station. They should look for other trucks that were strategically positioned around that area.

The two plus hours' drive out toward the truck stop had the tensions in the van at a peak. The drones were prepared and checked for readiness multiple times.

Lyle was quietly talking to Cathy and making sure she had her Kevlar vest on securely. He patted her as he put on her booties.

At the farm near the truck stop, Juan was with his men on the flatbed truck that they had prepared to shoot from. He had decided against any of them going into the woods that bordered a long pond that had been formed by the contractors that had built the truck stop. He wondered if there were any decent fish in it. He had the truck parked directly across from where the other three trucks would park.

He reminded them not to shoot any DEA agents or anyone that was shooting at the gunmen in the trucks. He reminded them of their three teammates in the bait truck. One of his men pointed out that they would not be able to shoot into that truck so the three were safe from all of them.

Ángel had decided to monitor the fight sitting in his office. He figured he was not needed and his Los Zetas gunmen could take care of themselves. His announcement of a one hundred thousand dollar bonus for each of them had gone over exceptionally well.

He preferred to enjoy the early morning with a café de olla and some Molletes, savor the open faced bolillo rolls topped with refried beans, melted cheese and pico de gallo. He was more into this style of leading from his office and chatting with his beautiful support that he had brought with him from Mexico.

She had brought in breakfast for the both of them. He was satisfied to watch from a camera that was mounted in the back of the trailer. He could see Emiliano standing at the ready at his fifty caliber machine gun and figured that the fight would not last long once the fifty got into action.

Jose had his Jalisco team revved up for the gun fight. He always got intoxicated by the adrenaline high that swept over him during a gunfight. The high stayed with him for hours afterwards. He had enough gunshot wounds that he had convinced himself that he would die an old man with his great grandchildren playing at his feet. He planned to enjoy this confrontation. He was going to stand next to Diego, his fifty caliber gunner, and enjoy the thunderous pulsing that it radiated. He was sure that the small band of DEA agents and the hired detective squad would be mowed down in short order. He just hoped that he got in some good shots.

Maximilian felt confident that he would be safe, but he had not taken any chances. He was wearing a top tier body armor that could withstand a thirty-ought-six magnum bullet. He was also going to stand to the back and let his men do most of the shooting. He figured the fifty caliber would end the fight before it even started. He had his limo follow the truck.

It would park in front of the truck stop and wait. Afterwards he would drive to his favorite restaurant for a late lunch celebration. He was thinking of a nice thick cut of rare filet mignon.

The three trucks, each from a different cartel drove up the ramp and into position in the parking lot just ahead of the bait truck.

Harold watched as three unmarked trucks, one pulling a blank white trailer, one that had a stainless steel trailer and the third that was a tarp cover trailer pull into three parking spaces. It was clear to him that these were most likely loaded with gunmen.

He let his team know and reminded them that as soon as the truck to be examined was pulled into position they should all get behind the rock filled containers.

When the truck they were following went up the exit ramp to the truck stop, Alex declared that they were the cheese in the trap.

The truck stopped as if to get gas. When the driver got out to pump gas two DEA agents arrested him. A third agent got behind the wheel and drove the truck to the designated offloading spot. Once there he jumped out and ran behind a dumpster to the front of the truck.

Trey drove slowly around the gas pump area. As they approached the back he asked Alex what she saw.

Alex took in the three parked trucks, spaced one truck space apart from each other and all of them aligned so they faced the offload area. She said she saw a trap that they needed to avoid.

Trey nodded and said that he was going to put the nose of their van up against the side of the first of the three trailers and they should get out from the side door closest to that truck driver's door.

Johnnie declared that he would take care of the driver if he was still in the cab.

Linda and Lorie said that they would be going to be right behind Johnnie and would launch their drones.

Alex pointed at Trey and said that she was following him out on his side.

Trey positioned the van and quietly said, "Go"

Johnnie rushed the cab of the truck and shot the driver as he was getting out with his gun drawn.

He heard the roar of the fifty and focused on getting his drone up and into the action. He flew his drone up so he could focus on the bait truck. He swooped in when the back door opened and shot the gunman operating the fifty. He continued in shooting anyone that had a weapon. He smiled when three men laying on the floor in the front of the trailer waved yellow hats at him. He turned his drone and shot his way back out of the van.

The many days of practice was paying off because he was able to shoot almost continuously as he exited the truck and then turned and shot the next gunman who had stepped up to the fifty. He was going to silence any shooter in the bait truck that dared to raise a gun. He soon had a silent truck.

Linda and Lorie had their drones up and were set to fire at the two vans on the other side of the one they were next to.

When the doors of those vans opened and the fifties started to fire they took their drones down and in. From their vantage point it was like they were shooting ducks sitting in a pond.

Each time someone stepped up to the fifty they shot them. The fifties were the main focus but there were other shooters behind the pallets.

Linda just kept swooping in and then flying up and circling back around. By the time she was coming back in a new person had stepped up to use the fifty. She shook her head because they made such easy targets.

Lorie had the canvas covered semi and had soon silenced the shooters that had ridden in on it by randomly shooting down through the tarp. The gunmen inside shot blindly upward but none got close to her drone. Her rapid strafing of the semi kept the fifty quiet and soon all shooting from the semi came to an end.

They all noted that gunfire was coming from the woods, but it was not aimed at any of the team. They would later learn that the Gulf Cartel had used the ambush to eliminate many of the other cartels gunmen.

Juan watched the bait truck being driven into position. He then saw the black van drive slowly in and put its nose gently against the side of the first trailer. He smiled at its position and knew that the shooters inside the three trailers were going to be in for a rude surprise when they threw open the rear doors and found nothing to shoot at. He was not sure how Alex's team would handle the fight, but it was clear they were not going to be surprised.

He then saw what he took to be drones rising up into the air. He watched as one of the DEA agents attached a rope to the bait trucks rear door and pulled it open as he took cover to the side. At the same time the rest of the DEA agents took cover behind two strategically positioned dumpsters. They were exposed to him but he was not interested in shooting DEA agents. He did not need a war with the entire federal government.

When the bait truck door opened, the roar of a fifty caliber machine gun firing immediately followed. He laughed because there was no one to shoot. He hoped the three men from the Gulf Cartel had stayed to the back of the truck and would survive the fight.

He was surprised a moment later when the back doors of the three trucks opened and the three fifty caliber machine guns started firing. The roar of four fifty's being fired at nothing was deafening and somewhat ironic to him. He shook his head and signaled his men to open fire.

He watched as five drones focused on the gunners of those fifties and killed them. He figured the fight would not last too long but the ones that had all the fire power would not be the ones that would win. He told his men to focus on the three trucks that had none of their buddies in them. He noted that the fifty in the first of the three trucks started up again and that it shot down one of the drones. He was amazed when he watched what happened next.

Trey was flying high and observed the fact that the DEA folks were exposed to the gunmen shooting from a flat bed, but they were not being shot at. He smiled as he realized that the shooters were likely the Gulf Cartel shooters who were not interested in shooting the DEA folks but were focused on shooting the competition who were in the trucks.

He swooped his drone down at the men on the flatbed and could see one of them wave to him.

He returned to the fight scene just in time to see Alex roll out from under the van, pick up what he figured was her drone and step towards the truck firing as she took each step. He also saw Cathy run and take a leap at a gunman who had rushed out to shoot Alex.

He swooped his drone in a kamikaze dive toward the entrance of that van firing as fast as he could. He flew in and continued firing until there was no longer the sound of gun fire. He crashed the drone wherever it was and ran to Alex.

Maximilian, standing in the back of the trailer was glad that he had not only worn his bullet proof vest but had thought of using hearing protection. The roar of the fifty seemed to shake the entire trailer with its sound. He was feeling heady about the ambush when suddenly a small drone flew into the van repeatedly firing as it came toward him. He raised his pistol to shoot when the world went blank. He had not counted on an expert marks lady putting a bullet between his eyes.

In the first trailer, Jose was stunned when the door opened and he had no one to shoot.

He was surprised when the fifty went silent and he realized that the gunner was dead. He stepped over to take his place, pulled the trigger and felt the surge of power flow into him. He was doing what he loved the most. He was dishing out death, but…, but…he couldn't find anyone to kill. Suddenly a small drone came towards him and he let the drone have it. He laughed as it went down just in front of him.

He suddenly saw someone pick up the drone, point it up at him and fire. He watched as the world slowly faded. He died laughing when he realized that he would not get to see his grandchildren after all.

A gunman with a AK 15 rushed out and was about to fire when he looked at his wrist and realized that the cracking he heard was a dog crushing it. Before the pain registered he died as a bullet hit him.

Harold had opened the door and dropped behind his dumpster. He soon realized that the gunfire coming from the field across from the truck lot was not aimed at he or his team. He focused on shooting the people in the three trucks that he could see. When things suddenly fell silent he cautiously stepped around to the back of the bait truck. He was surprised to see three yellow hats waving in the air and one of them yell out, "Gulf Cartel." He waved the three out with his gun. By the time they got on the ground his team was out and checking on the other trucks that had also gone silent. He told the three to run for the woods and join their buddies. He watched as they ran full speed and disappeared.

A few moments later he could hear a truck driving away across the field and he saw the rear taillights blink three times signaling their thank you. He once again marveled at the fact that for the second time the Gulf Cartel had come to the aid of Alex, the person that was known in Mexico as the "Black Angel from the North."

Alex had been hit by someone shooting at her from inside the truck when she took out the fifty, but her body armor had saved her. She knew from past experience that she would be sitting in the hot tub for the next week getting the pain to go down. She knew that she also had Cathy to thank for not having been shot by an AK 15 at blank range. She gave Trey a hug and thanked him for taking out the shooters inside of the truck.

He commented that he had nothing else to do since he was the number five drone and had been waiting in line for something to do.

She then went to the van and sat down on the step for the side door.

She looked up at the clear sky and the sun almost directly overhead. She smiled and let the team know that it was time for lunch, and she was treating.

9 The Reckoning

What I learned, as I listened to the whole recording of the battle at the truck inspection stop, shocked me. I got some of my earlier stuff I had shared wrong.

I listened to everything several times trying to get what had happened straight in my mind. The chatter on the way to the inspection stop made it clear that the team was anticipating a trap and they felt confident that the plan they had was the winning plan. Since I didn't know the plan I was left in the dark by the conversation they were having.

I heard my mother tell the team how they would know that the truck they were following was the cheese and they were thought to be the helpless mice. She pointed out that she and Harold had discussed how they would handle the situation and that his team was ready and prepared.

My mother voiced her concern about the fact that the semi that they were following had a fifty caliper machine gun mounted so that when the doors were opened it would be able to fire.

I looked up what a fifty caliber machine was like. I learned that it was a heavy machine gun that has been used by the US military for a long time and it is also known as the "Ma Deuce."

I had to look up why it had that nickname and found out that the Ma was for the size of the bullets it fired, the mother of all bullets, and the Deuce for the designation of the gun as an M2. In WWII it was affectionately referred to "mother F_ _ _of all machine guns." I guess that made sense to the soldiers that used it but it missed its mark with me.

What was significant was when I heard the four "Ma Deuces" firing at once. I had to take off my ear plugs and turn down the volume because I was sure that what I was listening to was how the end of the world would sound. I am amazed that the side firing those monstrous sounding weapons were the ones that lost their lives.

I shook my head when I realized that five small drones that carried one hundred rounds of nine millimeter bullets was taking on the "Ma Deuces." I looked up to see what size a nine millimeter was as compared to a fifty caliber bullet. The nine millimeter bullet could hide behind a fifty and not be seen. Not only was it smaller it was significantly shorter. I thought of it as the big bully and the brave defiant little guy.

The ability of the team to fly their drones and accurately shoot and kill the shooters in the van amazed me. It was clear to me that the defiant little guy was kicking butt.

What I was not prepared for were the pictures that one of the drones took of my mother rolling out from under a truck, picking up her drone that had been shot down, and using it to shoot at the person about to shoot her with the fifty. She staggered as she was hit but continued to repeatedly fire up into the trailer.

I saw Cathy leap into the air and then I could hear bones being crushed. I watched a shadow flew by and then I could hear the rapid fire of the drone's gun. I later learned that Cathy had saved my mother from being shot at blank range and that it was Trey's drone that met its fate in that trailer but not before it had killed every gunner in the trailer.

The next thing I heard was an EMT talking with my mother as she apparently sat at the side of the van where my microphone was located.

I had tears in my eyes as I could hear her faint moan as she was examine. I knew she was in pain and I wondered if I would ever be as tough she.

I was amazed that before going home to get in the hot tub she and the team stopped at the Golden Goose restaurant where they had lunch with me!

I listened to the five of them recounting the ease with which they had defeated the combined gunfire of three cartels.

I also learned about the supporting actions of the Gulf Cartel.

At that lunch I was clueless about what had happened and did not know that my mother had been shot. She acted as if everything was normal.

She even asked me if I had my homework done and after lunch she and I rode our bikes home. I didn't find out the details until the following day when I was cleaning the van and listening to what had happened the day before.

I don't know if I can continue listening to what my mother and her team do. They are all such powerful people and yet when I am around them I get the feeling they are the most kind and wonderful people. I don't want to say Jekyll and Hyde people, instead I essentially think of them of having contrasting personality traits across dimensions like risk taking and being extremely kind and social.

That sounds so much better than thinking of them a people with split personalities.

I now have a hard time being with my mother without wanting to repeatedly be giving her a hug !

*   *   *   *   *   *   *

As he took in what was happening, Ángel had almost choked on a bite of one of the Molletes. He took a sip of the café de olla as he tried to control the shaking of his hands. He watched as the men in his truck were rapidly killed one by one. The fifty caliber machine gun was almost useless because there was no one out in the open to kill. The area out in front of the fifties was empty. The first person on the machine gun was Jose, one of his best enforcers and he went down almost immediately. Every person who stepped up to take his place went down almost immediately.

The effectiveness of the armed drones were a surprise to him. He had never imagined such small devices could be so deadly.

Whoever was flying them was able to shoot them with deadly accuracy. He looked at his watch and realized that all thirty of his enforcers in the trailer had died in less than three minutes. Three minutes of hearing the roar of a fifty seem an infinity but he had only been able to take two sips of his café de olla.

He shook his head as he thought about the effect that would have on the money collection process and the ability to control his sector of Chicago. He hoped the other cartels had lost just as many enforcers otherwise he would be significantly outgunned.

The only silver lining he could think of was that the three million dollars that he had set aside to reward the men in the truck was still in his pocket and the other cartels would be as weakened as he.

Then it struck him that the Gulf Cartel had been in the woods. He wondered how many of them had been killed.

Juan was getting kudo's from his enforcers for having them on the truck across the pond. They at first had been worried they might face the fifties but soon realized that by being across the pond laying on the flatbed they were more like spectators sitting at a bull fighting ring watching a matador tease and kill the bull. They were not in the thick of things and they could concentrated on taking very specific shots that killed the enforcers of their competitors.

They also realized that it was almost as if they were watching five flying drones that were flying so effectively that those in the four trailers were literally sitting ducks and dying at an unbelievable rate. The display that the drones put on had all of them talking about the fact that they were happy not to have faced them.

They were surprised when as they were about to depart they saw Emiliano, Antonio and Juan waving their yellow hats and running their yellow shoes that did not seem to touch the ground as they ran to catch up to the departing flatbed. The three jumped onto the slowly moving truck and lay down panting but they had large smiles on their faces. They commented that they were the only ones that had lived through the gun battle.

They all rode along sipping on a Corona and singing "Besame Mucho", "Cielito Lindo" and "México Lindo y Querido". By the time they reached their warehouse the Coronas were gone and they all agreed that having lunch at restaurant "El Milagro," the miracle, was the place to go and afterwards they should all go to "La bebida del diablo," where the devil drinks, bar to continue their celebration.

Juan enjoyed the reaction that his men had and declared that he was paying for all of their partying. He knew that he was now in a dominant position in Chicago. He would send a note to the leadership team praising them for making such a brilliant decision.

The clean up at the truck stop was a macabre situation. The DEA team took in the situation and decided that the bodies would remain in the vans and they would all be driven back to the DEA evidence lot where the bodies would be individually identified and then sent to the morgue.

Harold noted that there were close to ninety bodies to process. He did a quick examination of each of the bodies and determined that the heads of the Sinaloa cartel and the Jalisco cartel were among the dead.

He let Alex know when he told her that she and her team should leave and that the DEA would handle the cleanup.

Alex was sitting on the step at the side of the van. She looked over to the two bullet riddled dumpsters that had shielded the DEA team. She took in the scarred surface of the parking lot black top where the fifties had repeatedly hit.

She thought about how the team had effectively handled the battle and had lost only two drones and she was the only one that had been shot. She thought of Johnnie saying, "money well spent."

She was holding her ribs where she had been hit. The DEA, EMS team came over to check her out and wanted to take her to the hospital. She put her finger in the hole that went through her pant suit jacket, her blouse and to the flattened bullet that had adhered to her Kevlar vest. She then shook her head and declined a ride to the hospital to be checked out and said that she was going home to sit the rest of the day in the hot tub.

She noted that her response didn't go over well with the EMT leader. She was familiar with that reaction because Matt, who had led an EMT team for most of his adult life, would have reacted the same way.

The EMT leader let Harold know about the decline. Harold came over and checked with her to make sure she was alright. He was well aware that this was probably the sixth or seventh time that Alex had been shot and that unless she was unconscious she never went to the hospital but chose to get to a hot tub.

He let her know that she and her team were free to go and the DEA would handle the cleanup and the follow up of identifying all of the dead. He let her know that the Sinaloa and Jalisco cartel leaders were among the dead.

Alex shook her head and said that she wondered what the number of dead enforcers and death of two of the Chicago based leaders would do to the drug flow into the Chicago area.

On the drive back she said that she was treating the team to a late lunch and celebratory drinks at the Golden Goose Restaurant. She said that she was going for a large, rare T-bone, mashed potatoes smothered in butter and grilled asparagus. She called ahead to see if Matt and Aurea wanted to join the team for lunch.

<u>10 Aftermath</u>

I have to tell you that I was not expecting to be in the thick of things. I had listened to everything that my mother and her team had done and to say I was impressed would be an understatement.

It affected me so much that it made me want to be as good as each of the people on my mother's team. That I knew was a daunting and almost impossible goal.

I had been saved by her. Linda, Laurie, and their mother had been saved by her. Johnnie claimed to have been given a second chance at life by her. I saw that Trey was devoted to her like no one other than my dad could be.

The people around her were great and I knew from the bottom of my heart that she was not only great, but she was the best person that I would ever know.

I knew I was a lucky girl.

She and I sat together in the hot tub, and she gave me a hug as if there was nothing bothering her. Later I learned that she was trying to ease the pain in her side where she had been shot.

What followed a few days later was a complete surprise to me, but I am proud of how I handled the situation. And the reason I was able to handle the situation was because my mother had prepared me to be able to do so.

Early one morning as I got off the school bus to go into the school building a man spun me around, pulled me along by the arm and showed me the gun he had in his hand. He told me to come along, and I would be OK.

He must have been daft to think that I would think that going with him was OK. He took me to a grey limo parked out by the street and pushed me in through the open back door. I could see another guy holding a gun on his lap patting the seat beside him. I got in and sat where he had indicated and the guy that had brought me to the car got in next to me.

No one said a thing. He quietly told the driver to drive to headquarters.

No one had to tell me that I had just been kidnapped.

It seemed to me to be right out of one of the mystery novels I had read. I also knew that I was going to be used to get my mother to do something that would endanger her life.

It was clear that they did not take me as a threat. They did not cover my head and they had all put away their guns.

I watched as we drove towards downtown Chicago. I had ridden by bike with my mother and father down the street we were traveling so I knew about where I was. I wanted to keep track of where they were taking me.

We arrived at a six story building, and I got the address number as we drove into the basement parking area.

We all walked over to an elevator and went up to the top floor. Then we walked down the hall to where a support sitting behind a desk, which was better than my mother had. She greeted us and said that Mr. Mayo was expecting them, and they should go right in.

I tried not to burst out laughing when she mentioned his name because I envisioned mayo spread on a piece of bread and the fact that my mother would probably be doing the spreading caused me to want to laugh.

Ángel watched as the young girl was brought into his office. He offered her the cookies and milk that he had Olivia prepare. He was not surprised by the fact that she turned it down. He asked if she knew why she had been brought to his office.

He watched her smile and reply, because he thought he was smart enough to outsmart her mother. He felt a sense of irritation as she continued and told him that he had no clue of the price he was about to pay for his misplaced belief that he knew how to handle the situation. She looked at him and said he should say his prayers and ask for help from above.

He was surprised at her self-confidence and willingness to challenge him. He smiled and told her that she was overconfident and that she was only an adopted child. He added that he doubted her adopting mother would come to her rescue. He had emphasized "adopted" to see if that would shake the girl up a little.

He was caught by surprise when she laughed and replied that the last two people who had challenged her mother's devotion were both pushing up flowers from six feet under. He then watched as she took a cookie, dunked it in the glass of milk, and asked what bakery had baked the great cookies that were almost as good as her adopting mother's cookies. He wanted to get up and slap the impertinent girl. He felt he deserved more respect from her than he was getting.

He was the one that broke her gaze, turned his chair, and looked out at the lake and told his two guards to take her to the main meeting room and keep her there.

Aurea followed one of the guards and the second guard followed her. When they got to the meeting room one of them took her backpack and took her phone out and put it in his pocket. He pointed to a chair and said that she should sit, be quiet and do her homework or whatever she wanted to do. She noted that he had not turned her phone off and smiled. She knew that he was ignorant of the fact that he was a homing beacon.

She flipped open her laptop, brought up her homework and behind it she connected to the internet. She typed off a quick message to her mother. "Kidnapped by Ángel Mayo - at his office."

She then got off the internet and focused on how she could disrupt the office area. She knew that she needed to give her mother time.

Disruption

She knew that her mother tracked the location of her phone and her computer, so she figured that soon "Mr. Mayo" would be getting a lesson on what messing with her mother really meant. She knew that she had to be sure not to get used as a negotiation piece the way that Mr. Mayo was planning to use her.

She needed to figure out how to be a disrupter like her mother.

She knew she was on the top floor and that there would most likely be other businesses that were not associated with the drug trade located on the lower floors. That meant that those people would not be of much help against the likes of the Los Zeta Cartel enforcers that were guarding her, so she was not going to try to go down.

She planned to use the fact that they thought of her as a helpless child to her advantage. She had worked especially hard at getting her first degree black belt. She felt confident she could take out both of her guards.

She had seen the guns the two carried and had identified them as the very good Five Sevens models. She had recently fired one at target practice where she watched her mother demonstrate its accuracy by shooting out the center of the target's bullseye. She had not been that good, but she had hit the bullseye three times as she fired the ten rounds from the pistol.

She knew that if she got one of them in her hand she would know how to use it. She had never shot anyone, but she also knew that she would do so if necessary. She was determined not to be a victim.

She figured that she needed to be like her mother and attack versus just standby or try to run away. She figured that she would wait for at least an hour so that her mother had time to figure out her attack. Then she was going on a disruption parade and shake up the floor as best as she could.

She was going to demonstrate to the Los Zetas Cartel what kidnapping her meant !!!!

*　　*　　*　　*　　*　　*　　*

Alex got the text from Aurea and at first went ballistic. She was ready to storm Ángel's office and put a bullet through his forehead. Her verbal reaction was loud enough that Trey was in her office almost instantly.

He asked her what had happened.

When she showed him the message she watched as he nodded, did not say a word and sat down. She could tell that he was deep into what he was thinking would be the way to get Aurea safely back.

He quietly said it was time for the team to finish dealing with the leader of the third cartel and take him out. He said they should spend a few moments thinking through how they should approach getting Aurea safely back and how to deal with the Los Zetas Cartel as they got her. He added that he had some ideas that might ensure her safe return while at the same time they did some significant damage to the cartel.

He then said it was time to get the team activated.

He went out, gave the van keys to Marisa, and asked her to bring the black van to the office parking lot. He then asked everyone else to meet in the large conference room.

Marisa knew that something very unusual was taking place when she was handed the van keys by Trey and he was the one calling the team together. This was the first time she had been asked to bring the van to the office or witnessed Alex following Trey into the meeting room. By the look on Trey's face, she knew what was taking place was going to get a response from a very angry Trey. She didn't know who that might be, but she figured it was curtains for that individual.

Once everyone was in the room Trey shared what had happened. He said that they needed to storm the building where Aurea was being held but they needed to do it in such a manner that they could safely extract her and then take care of the thugs that occupied the top floor. He was going to go up the fire escape and position himself at the top fire door exit. He looked at Johnnie and said that he was going to be the poor hungry vagrant that came off the elevator at the top floor and shoot anyone that he saw. He instructed Linda and Lorie to climb to the sixth floor on the east and west internal fire escape steps.

Once in position, they would all take action at the same time.

He looked at Alex and said that she was going to surprise Ángel Mayo by calling him and letting him know that she was on the way to pick up her daughter.

She would drive her Jag into the ground level garage parking and be taken up by the thugs that would come down to escort her. When she got to the top floor she would demand to see Aurea before she would be willing to do anything else.

Alex nodded and said that if she had Aurea, she would keep her safe.

He asked if everyone understood what to do. Linda smiled, said that she understood and that she was going to shoot every thug that she got a chance to shoot.

Trey nodded and said that as soon as they had Aurea then he wanted all hell to break loose. He smiled and said that everyone should be wearing their full Kevlar outfits. He then pointed as the black van drove into the parking lot and said that it was time for action.

Ángel was shocked when Olivia let him know that a person identifying herself as Alex was calling to let him know that she was on the way to pick up her daughter. He had not yet called to threaten to kill the impertinent daughter. He was now on full alert trying to figure out how the black bitch knew he had the daughter. He called his personal body guards and instructed them to meet her in the parking garage.

Alex drove her Jag down to the office building. She was certain that Trey's plan was a good one, but she was worried about keeping Aurea safe. She knew Aurea well enough that she would be figuring out what she needed to do. She hoped that Aurea did not get too ambitious.

As she drove into the parking area she saw the two guards waiting with their guns. One of them pointed to a parking spot where she parked. Neither of them said a word but both pointed to the elevator. She saw Johnnie standing in the shadows behind one of the square cement posts and knew he would be coming up behind them.

As she exited the elevator she pushed the button for the basement. The three of them were halfway down the hallway when she heard gun fire that she was not expecting. She dropped, spun, kicked the guard behind her in the knee and knew she had done the damage she had wanted when she heard the bones break and heard him scream.

She jumped up and placed a round house kick on the chin of the guard who was turning towards her. She heard his jaw shatter. He dropped his gun which she picked up and shot the guard behind her as he got ready to shoot her. The guard with the broken jaw tried to reach the gun dropped by his partner.

Alex shot him in the side of his head. She watched the elevator doors open and Johnnie come running out towards her. She turned and they raced down the hallway towards where she had heard the gunshots.

Aurea had waited for what she thought was a reasonable time and then she put her plan into action. She asked to go to the restroom. She was escorted by one of the guards while the other one stayed in the meeting room reading a magazine.

Once in the restroom she waited a moment and when she came out she stumbled as if she was going to fall but instead fell against the guard's side and pulled his gun from its holster. He threw her against the wall and had his fist in full swing to hit her, but she managed to flip the gun safety off and shoot him in the middle of his chest. He was about to fall on her, but she scooted over and let him fall where she had been. She knew she had killed him but did not have time to think about it.

She stayed on the floor as the second guard came out of the meeting room and raised his gun to shoot her. She shot him once in the chest and as he continued to raise his gun she shot him between the eyes.

Well almost. She noticed that she had missed and had shot him through his right eye. What was really gross was that she thought about a movie were a worm crawled out of the eye socket. She crawled forward so that she could use his body as a shield, but she couldn't get as close as she had hoped because of the amount of blood that was running out of his eye and pooling around the body.

So gross, no worm but so gross was all she could think about as the stream of blood kept coming out !

Ángel had just finished talking to his lead bodyguard as he got off the elevator when he heard the gunfire and wondered what was happening. Olivia ran into his office and said that they were under attack, and she had called for help and that there were at least eight of his enforcers in the office area.

He kept an AK 15 in the gun cabinet along with several pistols. He took it and a pistol out. He gave the pistol to Olivia and then loaded the AK. He figured that anyone coming through the door would end up full of holes.

He had not counted on someone coming through the window and was totally unprepared when the half inch thick bullet proof glass pane flew inward towards him and knocked him down. He looked up at what he was sure was a wild mad man that seemed to be flying in on the glass pane but had nothing but as small pistol in his hand. He laughed and was in the process of raising his AK when the world went blank.

Trey had been ready to enter through the fire door when he heard the two gunshots. He changed his mind and decided on jumping out on a rope from the roof and come in through the window in Ángel's office. He hooked his rope to the roof's edge and jumped. He came back feet first towards the window expecting the window to break and then he would roll in. Instead, the window stayed in one piece but flew in through the office. He rode the pane in like a surfer. The panel hit Ángel and knocked him to the floor. He had barely enough time to drop the rope, pull his gun, and shoot Ángel between the eyes. He pointed the gun at the woman who immediately dropped the gun she was holding and sat down on the floor.

He pulled her up by the armpit and pushed her out the office door.

Alex and Johnnie got pinned down in the hallway by two gunmen as they were running towards where they had heard the shooting. Her heart stopped when she spotted Aurea coming up behind the two gunmen. She almost fainted when Aurea shouted for them to drop their guns. As the two gunmen started to turn, she watched as Aurea shot each of them through the chest and then their heads.

It was a complete but welcome shock.

She got up and ran and hugged Aurea.

Johnnie ran past to the next hallway and began firing in that direction.

Linda had come through the stairway fire door and run into two guards that began to shoot at her. She was pinned in a doorway when Johnnie began to fire at the two guards that were standing in two separate office doorways across from each other. She lay down on the hallway floor and took out the first of the gunmen as he leaned out to fire.

Suddenly she saw Lorie appear from another hallway and run like a mad woman screaming at the top of her lungs and shoot the gunman who had stepped back into the office and was in the process of closing the door but had been too slow.

She ran forward and gave Lorie a hug and pulled her into the office where the dead enforcer was on the floor.

A few moments later Trey came towards Alex from one direction, Johnnie came from the other, Linda and Lorie joined them. They then methodically went from office to office and rounded up the bookkeepers, and other personnel and took them to the meeting room where Aurea had been held. By that time, they could hear the sirens and knew that soon the place would be overrun with police. Trey smiled and told everyone else to disappear and he would see them later at their second celebration luncheon.

Alex led Aurea down the fire steps by the elevator and had just pulled away from the building as the first police cars arrive. She drove slowly up along Riverside Drive, smiled, and asked how Aurea's morning had been.

She smiled as Aurea replied that it had been a little different than she had planned but it had been a very interesting morning.

10 Aftermath

11 Case Closed

My mother was quiet most of the way back to the marina. It seemed to me that she was talking to herself or trying to work through something. I figured that having me kidnapped had affected her more than she was used to having things affect her. I reached over, smiled, and used one of her lines on her.

"Smile, everything is going to be OK."

That got the laugh from her that I wanted.

She looked at me and said that she had never seen anyone as brave as me.

I shook my head and said that I had not been brave but I was mad and had decided to be a disruptor like my mother.

She nodded and said that the brave never realize how brave they are until someone else points it out to them and she was pointing it out. She put her hand on my cheek and said that she had the bravest daughter that anyone could possibly have.

I was glad that we got to the marina. The mother-daughter talk was getting to be too much to take. I now just wanted to have one of the great burgers that I loved.

When we got to the restaurant, I knew that word had gotten out about my kidnapping because everyone that my mother and I knew was there. The restaurant was full, and it had clearly become a celebration.

Matt gave me a hug and said that he was eager to take her fishing.

Trey came in with Lindsey. She came over and gave me a hug and asked how I was feeling.

I was feeling hungry and I had changed my mind about lunch. I wanted a small, rare porterhouse steak and a baked potato.

Trey came over and held up my arm and announced that he was holding up the hand of the person who had taken out the most cartel gunmen.

I was a little surprised.

He then picked me up and gave me a hug and whispered in my ear that I was as deadly as my mother, but I should take time to enjoy being young. Then he put me down and pushed me toward my grandmother. I went from one person to another getting hugs and being asked if I was OK.

Yes…Yes…Yes I was OK, but I was hungry.

I was about to say so when my mother rescued me and led me to a table where she, Matt and I were sitting by ourselves and a small, rare porterhouse was on the plate in front of me and the baked potato was on a side dish.

Matt put his hand on mine, smiled, commented that it was always hard to be the center of attention but added that I should enjoy it because it was one hundred percent better than being ignored.

I looked around at the people who had come for lunch and knew that I was a lucky girl to be the center of attention to the likes of the people that were there.

                    *   *   *   *   *   *   *

Juan arrived at his office to learn that there had been an attack on the offices of the Los Zetas and that Ángel Mayo had been killed. He called his informant that had a job with the Los Zetas and asked what had happened. He found out that Ángel had made the mistake of his life and had kidnapped the daughter of Alex Evercrest. The informant laughed and said that the daughter had personally shot and killed four of Ángel's enforcers. All of the top cartel enforcers at the office had been killed. He added that counting Ángel the Los Zetas had lost nine the previous morning.

Juan hung up and sat thinking about the situation. He had suffered no losses. All the other cartels would be trying to reestablish their organization with new bosses and new enforcers. It was his time to expand the Chicago Gulf Cartels control of the Chicago market.

He did not want to attract any attention so he would take it slow but would keep several steps ahead of the other three cartels. He knew he would have a good year or two ahead.

He called in his support and asked her to send out two bouquets of roses. One to Alex Evercrest and the other to Aurea Carvalho-Evercrest congratulating both of them for being the heroines of the hour but she was to keep anonymous who the flowers came from.

He wondered how the two would take the mysterious roses when they got them.

Alex was still nursing the bullet wound bruise on her side and had decided to spend the evening sitting in the hot tub. She smiled when Aurea joined her. She asked how she was feeling.

Aurea smiled and said that she was not the one sitting in the hot tub trying ignore the pain, she was there to enjoy the heat and ignore her mind that kept replaying the morning over and over.

Alex nodded and said that she understood. She shared that she had asked the team phycologist to come to the office in the morning. The phycologist would hold a team discussion about what had happened that morning and then have a meeting with each of them separately. She let Aurea know that she would have the first interview session and then she could leave and go out on the Golden Goose with her father and do some fishing.

Aurea nodded, asked about school and was glad to hear that her mother had arranged for a day off but had the assignments that each teacher was handing out. She figured she would do homework on the way out to the favorite fishing spot.

She hoped that talking to the therapist would help to put away the scene of blood coming out the eye of the second enforcer she had shot. That was the only scene that for some reason bothered her.

The next day Alex had the team meet together with the therapist. They were all gathered in the office lobby sitting in a circle.

Tracy had move to Evanston so she could continue her practice with the people she had found the most challenging. She felt great about the fact that she had regular meetings with the five people in Alex's office. She loved to listen to what the group did and looked forward to the sessions. She was surprised to have been asked to hold a group session that would include Aurea. When Alex shared the details of what had happened she wondered about the effect such an experience would have on a young girl like Aurea.

During the group session she listened as each of the team gave their version of what had happened. It was clear to her that rescuing Aurea had been the single focus of each of the team members.

She was impressed with how clearly Aurea expressed her experience and stopped to thank each of the team for coming to her rescue.

Later in a private session with Aurea she was even more impressed with the confidence and self-assurance of how Aurea held up her end of the conversation.

When she asked Aurea what bothered her the most about the experience she almost burst out laughing when Aurea said that she kept seeing a worm crawling out of the eye socket of the enforcer or a flow of blood come rushing out for her as she lay on the floor.

The worm was from a scene in a movie that she had watched. She couldn't recall the name of the movie or even the plot, but she recalled the scene of the magots crawling out of the eye socket. She asked Aurea to describe the scene. She smiled and said that she had watched the same movie and that she was remembering that scene.

Aurea suddenly laughed as she described the scene and then remembered hiding under her blanket watching that horror movie at night by herself.

She got up and gave Tracey a hug and said that now that she knew where that image was coming from she no longer was concerned. She had been worried that she was going crazy.

Tracey then asked why the flow of blood from the eye was also so vivid.

Aurea shook her head and said that she was not sure, but the amount of blood was more than she had expected, and she was mad that she had missed the shot between the eyes that she had intended. She said that she was sure she could now handle that scene since the maggots were no longer involved.

Tracey asked her final question. Who did Aurea think had sent the roses that she and her mother received the previous evening?

She was surprised when Aurea laughed and said that it was from Juan Ezequiel-Morales the cartel boss that was still alive.

Tracey asked why he would send both of them roses.

Aurea smiled and said that he had learned about her kidnapping and was being nice to her.

He had sent it to her mother because she was the "Black Angel of the North" and Friends with the "Angel on the Hill" that was in Mexico.

Tracey knew she had to figure out how to find out why Alex had that moniker. She asked if Aurea had anything else she wanted to discuss and when she got a no, she figured that it was time to let her go. She figured there were a few more sessions needed in the near term but that waiting and letting her go fishing was the best therapy.

She got a hug from Aurea and then watched her run out toward the marina.

When Alex came in she was asked how things had gone with Aurea.

Tracey gave a somewhat neutral reply and said that Aurea would do fine but should join the rest of the team in holding periodic therapy sessions.

She smiled and led in with the question about the roses.

Alex smiled and said that they had been sent by the Gulf Cartel boss and wondered why was she being was asked about them.

Tracey smiled and said that she had asked Aurea the same question and had received the same answer. She then simply said like mother, like daughter.

She then asked who the "Angel on the Hill" happened to be.

Alex shook her head and replied that she was a friend she had made several years ago and she was the reason that Juan Ezequiel-Morales the Chicago Gulf Cartel boss was alive and in the position to dominate the drug market in Chicago and to send roses.

That afternoon Alex got a call from Jane Stradford letting her know that she was declaring an end to the assignment and declaring a short term victory.

Alex asked what she should do with the five million that she had in her possession.

Jane said that she should bring it into the office and get a cashier's check for it so that there would be no question that the money that Evercrest, McGregor, Smith and Obrien Partners business took in was legal.

Later that day, Alex called the team together and said that she was splitting the money evenly with everyone that was a part of the business and the one young girl that had been part of taking down three major drug cartels.

She asked if anyone was unhappy with their share of that came out to be seven hundred and fourteen thousand dollars.

Johnnie laughed and asked who got the left over two thousand dollars.

They all laughed when Alex said that would just pay off the cost of the Kevlar bullet proof vest that she had given to Cathy.

"Money well spent," was Johnnie's final comment.

Alex closed the meeting and decided to walk over to the Marina so she would be there when the Golden Goose came back from what she hoped was a great fishing trip.

The End

Preview of: The St. Lebuinnus Church Murder

1 Life at the Top

Bas was enjoying the dinner with a view of the IJssel river. He had come across on the Ferry and walked down Lage Steen Way to the Meadow riverside restaurant where he was enjoying a lager and the view of the large white two deck party boat tied along the Quay on the other side of the river.

He had taken one of his many dates for an evening dinner and dancing cruise on that boat. The cruise and dinner had been better than the most of his dates. The date had achieved his objectives, but he considered most of them a little dull and had kept most of them to a one-night stand.

Now he was once again on the hunt.

He had been born and raised in Vlotbrug that was just south of Rotterdam along the Haring Waterway. He had spent many days fishing along the Forne Canal and riding his bike everywhere around the area.

It had been an easy and enjoyable way to grow up.

His parents were fairly well off and had encouraged him to pursue going to the university.

He had enrolled at Wageningen University where he had enjoyed the partying activities of the small university town. He found the curriculum associated with becoming a data analyst rather enjoyable and easy to fulfill. It gave him plenty of time to enjoy the pubs and soon he also realized that he enjoyed pursuing the opposite sex as much as having a good Pils.

He made it a point of enjoy almost an equal amount of each. His time at university had gone much too fast and now he had to produce enough at work so he would not get "ontslaged" or laid off.

He was sitting enjoying a Hieneken and thinking about his move to Deventer. He had taken a job with a startup, Piek Mooi Adviseurs (PMA) that was focused on supplying the region with customer eye, nail and beauty care preferences. His job was to organize, analyze and present the company leaders with information that would put them in position to advise their clients about how to best advertise and position their beauty care products. It was a role that he enjoyed, put him in touch with a variety of young professional women and mixed the social side with the technical data gathering programing side.

The two founders of the company were very beautiful women only a couple of years older than he. He was attracted to both of them but made it a point to not to mix work with his personal life activities. He kept his focus on doing his job and in doing it very well.

He made sure that he was doing that at the highest level possible and the feedback that he received from his clients corroborated that.

He took a sip of his beer and decided that he was going to make a move on the two women sitting a table away who were also enjoying a Pils. He purchase two at the bar and walked over to them.

He struck gold!

Later that evening as returned to his apartment he thought back over his short time in Deventer. He now felt very much at home in Deventer. He had found his role at work very satisfying, the city very comfortable and the young women that came to town on weekends very enjoyable.

It was, he felt a good life.

He walked around the corner, looked at the window displaying beauty care products and bumped into person doing the same thing. He began to apologize and then laughed as he realized that the beautiful lady was also apologizing for having been looking at the same beauty care products that he had been looking at.

His eyes met hers and he knew that they were going to have an affair. He took a chance and clumsily invited her for a bite to eat at one of his favorite restaurants near Wilhelmina Fountain.

She seemed to hesitated but then agreed to dinner.

Her name, Tess, seemed to him to be the perfect name for a very beautiful woman.

She was an inch taller than him but had a slender figure, long arms and legs that were meant for running. Her long flowing platinum blond hair that blew fluffily in a light breeze and her turquoise blue eyes froze him in his tracks.

He was captivated.

It turned out to be one of the more enjoyable dinners that he had in many a week. He found out that she liked to bike as much as he and they made a date to go on a Deventer–Markt Hattem round trip bike ride.

Bas was impressed with Tess's new light tan eggshell colored Gazelle Van Stael bike that she had purchased after landing her new job at her law firm. She had a black front pack where she carried food and a backpack where she had a small tent and some basic camping gear. He learned that she had taken several long rides where she had camped out.

He had also splurged on a new Gazelle Chamonix, but he had not outfitted his bike as thoroughly as Tess had done. He had taken several long rides but had not camped out.

He had on those occasions talked some attractive rider to spent the night with him at a bed and breakfast. He put those activities to the side as he focused on Tess. He very much wanted to get much closer to her.

Before their first ride, they met at the ferry and crossed over and then started on a seventy kilometer round trip. Their first stop was about six kilometers north at the Matanzas estate where he purchased tickets for a tour.

It was an enjoyable walk and afterwards they continued on some twenty kilometers and stopped at Veeessen where they took in an original windmill and ate a light lunch.

He was glad that he had thought ahead and purchased some bike-to-bike headphones that allowed them to chat as they rode. He learned that Tess had an eye for and knew many of the plants and flowers that they saw along the way. He also learned that she knew many songs with nature themes that she hummed or sang as she rode. Most were old nostalgic songs but a few he had recently heard by some current popular artists.

She mesmerized him.

Then late in the afternoon they made a brief stop for dinner and then they rode swiftly along the dike to reach Deventer before the sun set. They were both happy to see the main train station and then ride on to their apartments.

He would have loved to have ended the day spending the night with her but it was not to be. He sensed that she was not at moment seeking that type or relationship. He hoped that would soon change.

Winter saw the relationship continue to grow. Bas introduced Tess to cross country skiing but what they did the most often was to go ice skating at the De Scheg ice park. There he often hit the fast four-hundred-meter track to satisfy his desire for pure speed.

Out on the square, Tess had him holding her in his arms as she taught him to dance with her on the ice. He was a little clumsy but captivated by holding her and listening to her sing.

As the winter ended Deventer's pleasant temperature seemed to encourage every kind of flower to bloom. The reds, purples and a variety of yellow and orange seemed to open his mind to the beauty of the woman he as dating.

Tess spend every hour of an entire weekend going through Deventer's open-air book market, which he learned was the largest in Europe, usually held in the spring. He was impressed with the breath of her reading history and in her interest in both fiction and non-fiction. It was clear she was not into the romance novels. She had read all the world-famous writers.

He was certain that he had met the person who he desired to spend his life with. For the first time that he could remember he did not know how to make the next move. He was afraid if he pushed he might lose her.

The two of them took a weeklong bike tour through Norway during the summer. It was a breathtaking biking experience that began in Bergen, Norway and for seven days they rode north and stay at bed and breakfast inns. The fjords were a gateway to stunning natural beauty that was very different than the flat beauty of the Netherlands.

Several times they traveled by boat through the long fjords to get to the next part of the bike trail. The cascading waterfalls, the small idyllic villages, stave churches, hamlets and small farms all contributed to a breathtaking tapestry.

The experience deeply affected Bas and he was ready to commit his life to Tess as his lifelong companion.

Several weeks after their return, Bas was walking back from the market when he ran into Greta a voluptuous young woman that he had met and dated several times just prior to Tess. They literally bumped into each other as he rounded the corner.

He felt an instant sexual urge as she gave him a hug and suggested they have lunch.

During lunch Greta invited Bas to see her new apartment that she had just moved into. She was ecstatic about her new job as a chef at a local restaurant and the fact that she now would have enough money to afford some real vacations, not only in Europe but also a trip to the US.

He knew better but non-the-less he accepted the invitation. Greta led the way to her apartment and after a quick tour that ended up in her bedroom the scene changed.

Greta pushed him back on her bed and straddled his chest. It took Bas by surprise, but it had been a long time and his desires took over. He helped her take off her blouse and watched as her ample breasts with large areole and perky nipples bounced out as she giggled and swung them across his face.

He was ready.

She unzipped the shorts he was wearing and soon the two of them were naked on her bed. It was clear that Greta wanted to be on top and soon she was riding him. They spent the rest of the afternoon together in a round of sex, followed by a shower together and then a quick dinner in her apartment.

He ended up spending the night and left early the next morning. He knew that the whole encounter risked his relationship with Tess!

He returned to his apartment and prepared for a morning bike ride with Tess. He knew he would be in trouble if she ever found out about his tryst with Greta. He thought about how stupid he had been and swore to himself never to take such a chance again.

Tess seemed a little withdrawn, but they rode out together on a twenty-kilometer ride that had become common for them. They stopped for a lunch at a small countryside restaurant and enjoyed a light lunch. There was little conversation and Bas wondered what was up.

The following couple weeks Tess was busy with a case that she was handling and the two of them did not meet or go riding together.

Since this was different than what they had been doing, it worried Bas.

Then Tess invited him for dinner at a restaurant that she said had become her favorite because the new chef there prepared everything to her taste.

He was shocked and alarmed that her now favorite restaurant was the same one where Greta was the chef. Was it a coincidence or was it more than that?

He was nervous for the entire meal and could not concentrate. After a dinner and a walk arounds the edge of the old town and along the river, Tess invited him to go up in the Lebuinnus Church Tower where she had a surprise for him.

He followed her slowly up the stairs. She was wearing shorts, and her long legs triggered a desire for her that was more intense than usual. He really wanted to do more than just kiss her when they got to the tower platform.

Bas stood next to Tess watching as the sun was setting below the horizon in a glorious red and orange hue. He turned to look at her and was surprised to see the look in her face. He followed her eyes as she looked to the right and left beyond his shoulders then she smiled and asked whether his chef's body was better than waiting for hers.

Bas was shocked. He watched as Tess smiled, put her hands on his shoulders and pushed with all her might. He felt the rough stone of the railing as he slid over the edge and began his fall to the ground below.

2 Tess

*T*ess stood looking down where she had pushed Bas. It had all happened just as she planned. She had slowly come to love him, but she could not accept his betrayal. The betrayal had sealed his fate. She took one last quick look at his still and crumpled body as a shiver of excitement ran down her back. Then she stepped back into the tower.

She descended and took a furtive look outside to make sure there was no one watching. She then exited and walked slowly away on Nieuw street and then turned and walked to her apartment on Kuiper street.

She resisted looking back and focused her attention looking ahead. She was glad that there was no one out on the street. What took her somewhat by surprise was the sense of power, enjoyment and the warm feeling that she felt was better than sex go through her body.

There had been no one in sight when she pushed Bas over the railing, but she knew that it would not be long before he was found.

She walked at a slow pace to her apartment where after a long hot shower, she stood before the mirror, took in her slim figure, her accentuated breasts that looked to her like two slalom slopes, the she small brown spot just to the left side of her nose that was the only blemish in her otherwise smooth cream-colored skin. She knew she had a beautiful body. She had a trim figure and had often been hit on by various men.

Bas had never made the move that she had waited for!

She wondered why Bas had cheated on her?

She had hoped things would work out with Bas, but it had not been a hot romance. He was good looking, but she had considered him a little slow but over time she had grown to like him. She had been ready to make the move to get him into her bed.

She had hoped for a faster romance, but it had not happened. Then by sheer coincidence she saw him walking away with a voluptuous radiant looking auburn-haired woman. She discretely followed them and watched how Bas was reacting and holding her as they walked.

It was clear to her that the two knew each other well!

She followed them to the point where they both entered into an apartment building.

When Bas followed the woman into her apartment she knew that she and Bas were over.

She then spent time to learn more about the woman personally and discovered she was a trained chef that had just been hired at the restaurant Grand Friesian.

Then over several weeks she had frequented the restaurant to learn more about her. She learned that she was a local that had grown up, lived in Twello and had only recently relocated to Deventer when she had been hired as a chef.

She also learned that Bas had dated her for several years before the two of them dated so he had cheated on her with his previous lover.

Knowing all that had not helped and had instead sealed his fate!

She thought back over all the times she and Bas had spent bicycling, ice skating, dining on the river cruise, sailing and the fact that he had never made the move she had waited for.

It had made her wonder what his problem had been!

Bas's body was found early in the morning hours and because of the alcohol content found during the autopsy his death was considered an accident. There seemed nothing suspicious and there was no one to explain why he had gone up in the tower.

Tess sat at her desk and thought about the fact that she had planned and committed the perfect murder. It was a strange feeling that seemed to invigorate her.

She felt a new desire and began to look forward to the next good-looking guy that might hit on her.

She stayed focused on the law at work but now her biking took on a new focus.

She was thinking about where and how she would pull off the next successful murder, or as she though more about it, murders.

It seemed like the focus on the law was the salt that flavored the risk of once again killing someone.

It was a change in her that she had not expected but found that she was embracing.

She thought back to her school years and realized that she had always controlled the interaction with the male friends. She realized that controlling the men she had dated had always been part of her relationships.

She took to her new desire like a duck to water.

In her case it was a bike to a next murder location.

She studied the map and followed the IJssel north and south to scope out the locations she would pick to commit each murder.

She then rode her bike north along the IJssel and fifty miles south, located the places that she planned to take her victims and determined the methods she was planning to use.

It became her full time focus of hers after work activities. She felt exhilarated by planning the future events.

Her bike rides took on a new meaning. She took in the flowers, trees, the streets of towns and the flowing Ijssel with a new and thrilling perspective.

The Stadsgracht of Zwolle, a defensive star-shaped moat that surrounded the city with its centuries long history as a defensive moat immediately attracted her. She was impressed that the Stadsgracht was constructed around eight hundred AD by Frisian merchants, the troops of Charlemagne and that it had received city rights in twelve thirty from the Bishop of Utrecht.

It had a long history as a trading city at the point where three rivers converged, and the city flourished. Tess rode through the city and located all the interesting shops and night spots.

She contemplated the moat and decided that she would stage a swim-drowning.

She found the night spots that she planned to frequent to meet her next lover victim.

She looked south for the next location and picked Nijmegen because it had the Charlemagne connection and the fact that it was the oldest city in the Netherlands. Charlemagne had built a palace on the Valkhof, a hill overlooking the city.

She was planning her event not on the hill but a drowning that would feature an improperly worn life jacket. She realized that she would need to match her dates with the type of death she was planning for them.

Now when she stood before the full-length mirror in her bathroom she would smile as she thought about the queen in Snow White standing before the mirror and finding out that Snow White was the most beautiful woman and then giving her a poisoned apple to kill her.

Snow White had been saved by a good fairy who put a spell on her that put her to sleep until kissed by a true love.

She had found out that Bas had chosen another woman over her and her response was to put him to sleep forever.

He would have no true love's kiss to bring him back to life.

She looked back into the mirror and asked herself how many poisoned apples would she hand out.

She continued to identify the locations where she would carry out her deeds. To the south in Hoven, she planned another death where she would stage the scene where a bikers pants caught in the chain causing the rider to drown.

To the north at Langen Kulk, she planned a swimming-drowning.

To the south at Apeldoorn, it would be a drowning in the water in the bottom of a boat.

The Kanaal Zuid would be the site of an inner tube drowning.

To the East at Harder Wijk it would be a paddle board fall where the paddle boarder head hit his head on a rock.

Then to the West at Coevorden there would be a suicide fall from a giant electrical power generation windmill.

This was a scene that had captured her imagination. She would climb up ahead of her lover to be but what he would receive at the top was not what he was looking at as he climbed up behind her.

Tess rode her bicycle to each location to see where she would commit the murder. Over the year she put in countless miles.

She thought about putting in some winter deaths but struggled with the logistics of the cold weather deaths.

She was surprised at her personal mental condition as she thought about what she was doing.

She felt fine but she also realized that she was about to undertake a personal project that would make her in to a person who would be referred to as a black widow.

This thought was tantalizing and attracted her !!

She stood naked before the mirror and admired her lithe body. He bicycling and her daily workouts had her in top physical shape. She had the six pack that was always referred to.

She began to fill her closet with the clothes that she planned to use as the lures that would attract the men she planned to do in. The selection of clothes were very different than the ones she wore to work or had previously kept in her closet. Each day she would spend a few moments pulling them out and admiring them.

She decided that her victims should be men from the locations where she planned to kill them.

To accomplish this, she identified the night spots in each location and began to frequent them.

Her hunt slowly yielded the men that seemed eager for one-night stands.

She actually enjoyed the hunt and figured she had several exciting years of fun ahead.

She also enjoyed the variation that she experienced as she took in the slightly differing norms from one region of the country to the other and the differences in the men that she was selecting.

She smiled as she thought about the phrase, "variety is the spice of life." It certainly was the spice that caused her body to react when she was out on the hunt.

In the first year she created what she thought of as the four corners of the cross she would forever bear. She killed four unsuspecting men that desired her body but instead were lead to their deaths.

In Zwolle she had met and culled out Ted with whom she slept several times and learned that he was isolated from his family because of a fight with his stepfather. On his fateful night, she spiked his drink and then got him to go swimming by taking off her clothes and luring him into the waters of the Stadsgracht. She was able to push him under and hold him down until he drowned. She then got out, dried off, got dressed put a suicide note on his phone, returned to her car and drove home.

Once home, she enjoyed a hot shower, dried off, stood in front of the mirror and admired her lithe body. The feeling that coursed through her body send a shiver up her back that made her shake. She smiled into the mirror and thought that it was better than any sexual feelings she had ever experienced.

After the first kill, she knew she was on the way. She had felt a surge of desire and then the after effects that traversed and shook her entire body.

She tried to find out how that death was reported. It was a very short report on a suicide in the moat.

For her next kill, she developed a relationship with Len a handsome professional to the south in Nijmegen.

She used a similar approach with Len with whom she spent several nights.

He too had no family connections, and she made it a point of not meeting any of his friends. She had him very drunk when she walked with him to the canal, put him into a life jacket and pulled him out into the waters of the canal. She turned him face down in the water until he drowned. She then left him face down in the water and left the scene.

She returned home and once again lingered under the hot shower, leisurely dried off and admired herself in the mirror. She felt the surge that went through her body and knew that she was reaching ever heightening surges that coursed through her body. She continued standing before her mirror, reliving the killing and enjoying the same exhilarating feelings.

The report in the local newspaper highlighted the fact that the life jacket had been put on in fashion that facilitated the drowning. No foul play was suspected!

She spent a good month improving her paddle board skills in preparation for her next kill in the east at Harder Wijk.

There she met Ralph who qualified by being a loner that spent his time paddle boarding and having an occasional beer at a canal side café and bar. She convinced Ralph that a moonlight outing would be very interesting and exciting for him.

She didn't lie. She spiked his beer at the bar and then led the way to the canal. Once away from the bar she stopped where the banks had been lined with head-sized stones.

There she got off and when he sat down, she hit him across the forehead with a stone.

She positioned his body as if he had come in toward the shore, hit the rocks and then flew head first into the rocks.

She picked up her board and carried it to her car, secured it and drove away.

It was a full day later before Ralph was found.

His death was attributed to his drinking, hitting a rock and dying of a concussion.

The coroner's report highlighting the fact that he could have been saved if he had been brought to a hospital. That information sent a shiver of pleasure through her.

It was the message that her body had been awaiting.

She next pursued Peter a tall handsome blue-eyed mountain climber, bicycle rider, adventurer. He was probably the most attractive to her of the three that she had scheduled to fulfill the cross that she was in the process of creating.

The accident she planned for him was as frightening to her as it was special!

She determined that Peter would commit suicide by jumping off the top of an electrical power windmill.

She had climbed to the top and determined that it had an area large enough to have a picnic at the top.

The climb up had almost discouraged her from her plan, but she had decided that it was a kill challenge she felt the most excited about.

Just thinking about it had caused her multiple pleasure surges.

She chose a moonless night and then let Peter know that there was a special treat for him when they got to the top.

She led the way wearing a short, short skirt that had nothing underneath. When they reached the top she spread a blanket, and they engaged in sex.

Then she put out as picnic treat that included a beer that she had spiked. Once Peter finished the beer, she finished Peter by pushing him off the platform and watching as he flayed his arms and legs on the way down.

The height of the windmill was high enough that she did not hear him hit the ground.

When she climbed down she walked over to where he lay and relished the fact that his body had literally splashed into the ground as if it was Jello. The note she had left on his phone at the top of the windmill simply said, "I can't put up with all the pain in the world."

Her drive home was a continuous cycle of pleasure surges. The shower and mirror ritual was so overwhelmingly pleasurable that she wanted to embrace and hang onto the feeling forever.

She could not remember any of the legal work that she had done for most of the year and when she was praised for the excellent work she had done she had to review the cases she had worked on to remember any of them.

The four points of her death cross had taken her more than a year to accomplish. She was looking forward to the next four that she had planned for the following year.

The hunting for suitable men was as much fun as the killing was exhilarating. She entered the next phase of her journey with energy and high expectations.

Thanks for reading this far; To finish the previewed to story go to:

https://www.remwriter95.net/

About the Author

Ronald E. Mueller
remwriter95@gmail.com

Ron grew up in what is now Flint River State Park in Southeast Iowa. The 170-year-old house Ron lived in is built into a hillside. It faces a 125-foot-high cliff towering over the little Flint River. The house and the land talked to him about; the passing of time, the struggle to conquer the land, the struggles people faced and the wonder of nature.

He climbed the cliffs, crawled into the caves, dove from the swimming rock, collected clams from the bottom of the pond, gigged and skinned frogs for their legs. He trapped muskrats for fur, hunted raccoon in the dead of night, and with only a stick hunted rabbits in the dead of winter.

His young life was outdoors, and nature tested him.

He walked to a one room stone schoolhouse uphill both ways. A stern but warm-hearted teacher, Mrs. Henry was instrumental in shaping his character as she shepherded him from the fourth to the eighth grade.

It was a great way to grow up.

Ron graduated from Burlington, High School, went to Vietnam in the Navy. He graduated from The University of South Florida with an master's degree in engineering, worked for thirty eight years for Procter and Gamble, traveled around the world thirty times.

He has remained happily married for more than fifty years. His daughter and his two sons are all successful and his three grandchildren have all graduated.

His wife has humored and supported him as he became a full time became a professional story teller.

His experiences inter-twined with snippets of fantasy lend themselves to the adventures he leads the reader through.

Science Fiction
The Savitar Series:
Journey's End
Savitar
Confluence
Savitar Series Collection

Bram Nielson Series
The Fold
The Message
Fold Wormhole
Negative Fold
Ripples in Time
Bram Nielson Collection

Single Science Fiction Books:
Current Past and Future
The Event
The Door
Viajante 7

https://www.remwriter95.net/

Characters in the Story

Alex	Cathy	Evercrest	Cinci Police Detect to private practice
Matthew	Timothy	Knolton	Alex's suitor
Aurea		Carvalho	Daughter Adopted by Alex
Rose-Anne	Germain	Evercrest	Alex's mother
Russel	Johnson	Evercrest	Alex's father
Trey	Clay	McGregor	Alex's Detective Partner
Lindsey		McGregor	Wife
Nolan		McGregor	Son
Johnnie	Baily	Smith	Black Vietnam Vet.
Mary		Higgins	Johnnie's Philadelphia "friend"
Jane	Elousie	Stradford	Lieutenant Governor
Bruce	Lincoln	Johnson	Cincinnati Chief of Detectives
Mary-Anne	Leslie	Johnson	Chiefs Wife
Bill	Hamilton	Danson	Detective
Travis	Bailey	Carter	Detective
Jane	Elousie	Stradford	Lieutenant Governor
Jesse		Franklin	Chicago Police Department Chief
Dexter,			Previous owner of the dock area
Annie	Lorie	Scots	Missing girl Married Brian O'Neil
Linda		Scots	Annies older daughter
Lorie		Scots	Annies second daughter
Darrel		Quinly	Pilot of the private jet Brian leased.
Brenda		Langely	Art Dealer
John	S.	Williams	Lawyer that was abused
Hanna		Waverly	John's mate
Angelica			Angel on the hill
Ernesto	Jesus	Caldero	Gulf Cartel Boss
Adriana	Maria	Calderon	Ernesto's Wife Nea; Ramirez
Adolfo			Angelica's brother
Alejandra		Rumerous	Adolfo's wife to be.
Cais		Leu	Alex's Viet friend
Tracy		Hunter	The analyst in new office
Jason		Shephard	Alex's first boss
Rupert		Quinlin	Bus converter
Harold		Zimmerman	DEA
Lyle		Dilansky	DEA dog handler teamed with Cathy
Janaina		Carvalho	Mother
Aurea		Carvalho	Daughter Adopted by Alex
Bento		Carvalho	Father
Marisa	Kimberly	Eberly	Support Alex's Detective Practice
Capt. Bilan		Kirpatrick	Captain at the San Diego Naval Base
Riley		Lansberry	Pilot, Alex's new company plane

Knolton's Golden Goose Marina and Restaurant
Evercrest, McGregor, Smith and Obrien Partners, LLC

Golden Goose		Name of the Yacht
Gunjfor		Name given to gun totting hover craft.
Maximilian	Campo	Chicago Drug Distribution boss for Sinaloa Cartel
Jose	Alfredo	Chicago Drug Distribution boss for Jalisco Cartel
Ángel	Mayo	Chicago Drug Distribution boss for Los Zetas Cartel
Olivia	Becerra	Los Zetas support to Angel
Juan	Ezequiel- Morales	Chicago Drug Distribution boss for the Gulf Cartel

161

https://www.remwriter95.net/

Published by: Around the World Publishing LLC.

www.ingramcontent.com/pod-product-compliance
Lightning Source LLC
Chambersburg PA
CBHW070547100726
47907CB00004B/1305